All He Wants For Christmas is a Fingerling

The Weird & Wacky World of Shifters

Book Cover © 2021 Design by Tina Løwén
People in images are models and should not be connected to the characters in the book. Any resemblance is incidental.

Editing by Lucas Cornelius
Proofreading by Abbie Nicole
Book Formatting by Tina Løwén

References to real people, events, organisations, locations, or establishments are only intended to give a sense of authenticity and have been used fictitiously.

The author acknowledges the copyrighted or trademarked status and trademark of any goods, iMac, AMC Rebel.

Films, music, and lyrics mentioned are the property of the copyright holders.

Warning
Some of the content of this book is sexually graphic, with the use of explicit language and adult situations involving two males. It is only intended for mature audiences.

ll He Wants For Christmas is a Fingerling

MM Shifter romance/opposites
attract/MPreg/Grumpy & Sunshine/Weird Shifters

An errand leads Tala to the mate fate has chosen for him. Frenchie is nothing like Tala expects or thinks he wants. Can love and the universe make Tala see sense before he ruins any chance of a happy ever after?

Tala has the life he wants. His brother leads the pack and deals with all the pesky details of their joint auto shop, leaving him to tinker with the cars. Life is just the way he likes it.

In the blink of an eye, his entire world turns upside down when he's forced to enter the twilight zone of weird and wacky shifters. If that wasn't bad enough, the inconceivable mate leads him down a dirt road to unexpected happiness. Only the road has bumps. Two, to be precise, and the big wolf is going to learn just how hard it is to keep his seat with a hormonal mate.

Dedication

This book was inspired by a poll and created for Julie (aka Jess) who encouraged me to write an MPreg shifter book.
This one is for you Julie for all its weirdness, I know you love Tala and Frenchie.

Merry Christmas to all

Chapter One

Tala

The dirt road I'd been traveling seemed to go on forever. Heat shimmered in the air, and the tiny amount blowing through the window I'd opened did nothing to stop me from sweating. Why did it have to be so damn hot nearly all year round? It was two months till Christmas, shouldn't there be fucking snow or something? Maybe I should move to Alaska? Wasn't there snow there?

I swiped my bangs off my forehead. They kept falling into my eyes after the hair attempted to glue itself to my forehead. I squinted at the never-ending dirt road I'd been on for what felt like forever, watching for a sign that would tell me I was nearly at the godforsaken town I was looking for.

"Why did I have to be a do-fucking-gooder?" I bitched aloud, knowing full well I wasn't that at all. There was nothing but shimmering air, miles of empty dirt road, and fields on either side of the truck that appeared to stretch on forever.

I'd lost count of how long I'd been sitting in the truck, but my ass was numb and I'd long lost my patience. I mean, sure, I had hardly any patience to begin with. Many would attest I was a grumpy

7

fucker who mostly preferred my own company. It's why I'd initially been happy—sort of—to do this errand.

How's that turned out for you, dickhead?

Right now, I could be in my cool cabin deep in the woods, scratching my balls, watching shit on the TV, and slugging back a cold one. My brother was going to fucking know what it was like to have a true fucking pain in his ear when I got back. His fucking bullshit about how this would be an easy trip, which could be done in a day, had faded about six hours ago.

Lying fucker!

I should have insisted he send one of the sniveling betas. They were always looking to suck up to the alpha. Not that the omegas were any better. They were forever crying to Olowin about the way I talked. Calling someone out for shit they did, what the fuck was wrong with that? Fuck it all in my estimation, which was why I'd chosen to build my cabin away from the pack. It also meant I wouldn't be asked to get involved in any of the day-to-day shit that someone always wanted help with.

My omega papa had successfully birthed twin boys, both alphas. It was my bad luck to have popped out first. For eighteen years, I'd been joined at the hip with my twin brother while we trained together to lead and fight for the pack because that's what my father had wanted. Born several minutes apart, there'd always been pressure and expectations about my future. Which

I'd avoided talking about, expecting, like most, that my father would have a long lifespan, much like his ancestors. Only he'd died because he was a stubborn-ass fool who hadn't listened to reason or the doctors until it was too late. He'd contracted wolf fever, a nasty thing that fucked up the heart and lungs. His death had devastated my omega dad while the rest of the pack had looked to me for leadership.

Selfishly, the ole man dying had not been part of my life plan, not that I had one. The pack council seemed to think that they could alter that by giving me a plan. Being the oldest alpha son, in pack law, they were always the one next in line to lead. I'd quickly set them straight. It wasn't going to be me. My twin brother Olowin had a temperament much better suited to dealing with the pack. He at least could control his temper and his mouth.

The argument had continued for hours until they'd realized I wasn't budging, and because I was the most powerful alpha in the pack, they'd finally relented. The one proviso was that I didn't leave the territory, that I'd be there to support my brother. That part had been no problem as I hadn't planned to go anywhere. I liked the little part of Texas we lived in, bar the heat, and that really didn't bother me that much. Sort of.

The problem was shit like this, where I ended up forced to pick up the slack in our joint business when Olowin had to deal with pack issues, which there was always a mountain of. Days like today were becoming far more frequent, and I'd be the one having to drop what I was doing to go get the parts we needed when weird-ass places in the back of beyond didn't have a pickup delivery service. I mean, in this day and age, who the fuck doesn't have a system to send shit across the country?

Yeah, when I'd looked to find Potatoville on the map, I hadn't been able to find it, so I suppose that could be difficult. It was weird that it wasn't there, and for a while, I'd considered it might have been a prank someone was playing on me. But the person I'd been emailing had sent photos of the transmission for a nineteen-seventies AMC Rebel, which dispelled that idea. In the end, I caved and asked for directions.

As I stared out the dirty windscreen, I was starting to think that they'd sent me on a wild goose chase. One I'd be mightily pissed about. If that were the case, and I'd traveled hundreds of miles to buy a transmission that didn't even exist, someone would pay.

Fur bristled through my skin, and I tampered back the anger that brought my wolf to the surface. I pressed my foot to the accelerator, shifting my ass on the leather seat, hoping against hope I'd see something soon. It had taken months of searching to find this part, so I wasn't giving up just yet. I'd promised the customer, a wolf from another pack, I'd have his car ready by Christmas, and I planned on keeping my word.

Our auto motor shop specialized in fixing-up rare American muscle cars. The Rebel I was working on right now was a thing of beauty. I'd lovingly restored the body work and, even if I do say so, it looked as good as the day it rolled out of the factory. Now all that was left for me to do was fit the transmission, which I'd stupidly thought I'd be doing this evening. Only the place I was looking for was far harder to find than a bloody needle in a haystack.

I was in the middle of fuck-all-ville, never mind Potatoville.

Was it really called that?

The potato crops on either side of my truck showed why they might have named a town that, but it was still a stupid ass name. Who comes up with shit like that?

Distracted, the truck bumped over a large pothole, and I cursed long and loud as my ass left the seat, and I bounced up, striking the top of my head on the roof of the truck. My vision was obscured for a moment as my bangs fell in my eyes. The top of my head throbbed as I swiped at my hair, blinked, and slammed on the brakes.

Outside the truck, my tires screeched across the tarmac. The seatbelt dug into my large chest and my heart jammed itself up into my throat as I stared at the tiny...man—and he was tiny—standing at the side of the dirt road. I blinked several times to confirm I hadn't lost my marbles from the strike to the head because the guy sure as hell hadn't been there a second ago.

I glanced about.

Where the fuck had he come from? There was nothing for him to have appeared from behind. Had he been crouching down?

My gaze swept over him. On first impression, I'd have said he was young, maybe a teenager just because of his small size, but there were lines around his eyes that indicated he was older, maybe in his twenties. He had to only be around five feet, wearing ragged shorts and a T-shirt, both in brown, and his feet were bare. His legs and arms were a golden brown that matched his tangle of gold-threaded brown curls. Brown was my first impression. He blended with the dirt, somehow, with the exception of dirty, gold-streaked hair and eyes that were...the palest of blue. Crystal clear like the waterfall that was hidden on my land. There was an intensity to the stare that was unnerving, especially when he didn't blink, not once.

A buzzing started in my ears as our gazes met and held, and I got an odd warming sensation in the center of my chest as my wolf yipped in excitement. My hands balled in my lap when I got the strangest urge to...fuck knows. Whatever it was, it was weirding me out.

There was nothing about him that stood out, yet for some unknown reason, I couldn't look away. My wolf surged forward as if preparing itself for something. Was I missing a threat here?

Staying where I was, I tilted my head closer to the open window and sniffed the air. My wolf got all giddy while I couldn't for the life of me identify what kind of shifter he was. Nonplussed and more than a little pissed that I was struggling to keep control of my wolf, I sniffed again. Still the same dirt and maybe...something sweet?

My gaze narrowed suspiciously.

He was too far away and standing barefoot in the dirt. Did that mask his scent in some way? There were so many diverse kinds of shifters, and most kept to their own kind. I'd considered that I'd be traveling to another wolf shifters territory, and I'd identified who I was before I'd come. Now that I thought about it, there'd been no mention of what kind of shifter was selling the transmission. Had I wrongly assumed it was a wolf?

I released the seatbelt, keeping my gaze on the man in front of me as I left the truck idling. Not that I was worried, I could defend myself in either form. The moment my boots hit the ground, a feeling of...peace and serenity rolled up through me. Used to always feeling pissed about something, the change was notable and set my pulse to skip several beats. Was there some fucked up shit in the dirt to make shifters defenseless?

That thought made the situation weirder. The guy didn't appear to realize I was an alpha or drop his gaze, as was customary. "Yo. You know where Potatoville is?" I rasped in a growly voice.

His eyes never blinked, unnerving me as he pointed down the road I'd been traveling. Taking a deep breath didn't seem to help the oddness of the feelings flowing through me with my wolf lying on his back, his belly exposed.

Jeez! I wasn't in Potatoville, more like fucking weirdsville!

With more trepidation than I'd ever admit to, I walked to where the guy remained. The scent of dirt increased, but the other element I hadn't been able to place inside the cab got stronger. Nah, I must have been baking my brains in the cab of the truck too long. How the fuck can he smell like my favorite fries covered in ketchup.

I barely had time to shake off the silly notion when my head was filled with whining, which quickly turned to howls when I stopped within a few feet of the guy. My wolf was not happy that I wasn't getting closer.

What was this nuttiness? I must have entered an alternative universe because I was clueless as to what the fuck was happening or what was making my wolf act so damn crazy. My mouth filled with sharp fangs as my gaze swept the area, looking for what was causing my wolf to react. Heart pounding at no obvious threat, my gaze returned to the guy who remained where he was, acting unconcerned.

What was his game?

I was forced to close the distance reluctantly when my wolf wouldn't quit, giving me a damn headache. Sweat slid down my spine in an effort to keep control over my animal. My hands balled into fists, readying to fight whatever was setting off my wolf even as the peaceful feelings pushed against the need to protect...but protect what?

"What are you?" I demanded when I was within touching distance.

A smile as bright as the fucking sun blinded me, and my wolf's excitement increased.

"A Fingerling," he sang in a strange voice.

My brows arched, and using my alpha power, I growled, "Seriously, I won't ask again. What are you?"

The smile got bigger, and with it came a sense of knowing that got my stomach fluttering with...

"Yours."

Involuntarily, I stepped back.

No fucking way.

It can't be.

No.

No way in hell!

Another step back, and my wolf lost his shit as the guy's smile disappeared and what appeared to be a look of devastation followed. But I didn't get time to find out why when the guy vanished into thin air. I blinked owlishly, putting my hands on the sides of my head as my wolf howled inconsolably, deafening me.

Give the fuck up with that. I can't concentrate.

My wolf growled, paced in my mind, but stopped the howling giving me a chance to acknowledge what the fuck had just happened. Or not, because there was no way that...*disappearing thing* was my mate!

Chapter Two

Frenchie

Hurt cut deep at the rejection as the truck disappeared off in the direction of town. Why had the wolf not acknowledged I was his mate? Was I so repulsive?

I mean, I was tiny next to the big alpha wolf who had to be a foot and a half taller than me. I suppose he could think I was weak. I wasn't. I might be short and wiry, but I was strong. Okay, I didn't have all the bulging muscles that he had stacked everywhere. The T-shirt and low-slung jeans he wore didn't hide the power in his body. The thick dark hair and beard were...

I rolled a little in the dirt, hoping it would cool my skin, which was heating up from where my thoughts were heading. I'd a very vivid imagination, and I was sure the wolf would be hairy...everywhere. Rolling all over the top of his body would be...yummy.

Ew, stop that! We don't need to hear those kinds of thoughts!

He got rejected. That's all he's got, so let him be.

It was a wolf, and a big one, who'd want that as a mate.

My brothers all talked over the top of each other, vying to be heard, which didn't normally bother me, but right then, I didn't want to hear it. Not when I hadn't had time to prepare—not that one could prepare for meeting their mate without prior warning—so I could have made a good impression.

You'll get us into trouble with the elders thinking about this stuff! My elder brother hissed.

Leave me alone.

I closed off the part of my mind that allowed me to communicate with my family in my potato form. I didn't need them listening in to my thoughts right now or telling me what a failure I was when I was still devastated at being rejected. The elders had made finding a mate sound wonderful, although they'd always implied it would be another potato who'd be my mate, not a big wolf.

Had I got it wrong?

Mixed things up?

No, I'd felt the tug, and my cock had never reacted the way it had to the scent coming off the wolf. Shifting over the dirt at speed, I rolled toward town, the need to see the wolf, even if he didn't want me, compelling me forward.

Had the elders, who'd said it was all nonsense to think we'd be mated to another species due to our uniqueness, been mistaken? I know I'd daydreamed about who would come and rescue me from living my whole existence with other potatoes and the boredom of harvesting potatoes. Had that got me imagining something that wasn't true? The doubt warred with the part of me that was convinced the wolf was my mate.

Maybe the wolf didn't know he could be mated to something like me? Was that it? Had he been confused?

My heart sank—not that it could get much lower to the ground in my potato form—as I recalled his pissed-off expression. There'd been no confusion, just pissed-off-ness. Why had the elders never mentioned that a true mate could reject his chosen one?

It was all so damn confusing. I picked up the pace, hoping the magic in the dirt would soothe my raw feelings. Whenever I was hurt or upset, I would come to the fields and roll about in the dirt. It always helped to make me feel better. Right now, there was a fifty-fifty chance of it working when all I wanted to do was change into my human form and demand the wolf...

The sigh in my head was loud and heartfelt. No one could force another to take what they clearly didn't want. I'd had no intention of revealing myself when I'd heard the sound of the truck, none whatsoever. Nope, I wasn't at all intrigued to see who was passing through.

Liar!

It wasn't just that it was a rarity that someone drove through these parts unless they were lost. There had been something sparking inside me that got me to reveal myself when I scented him. I wasn't mistaken. That feeling had been real, as real as any I'd felt.

Another sigh, and I considered why he was driving in this part of the country. Asking for directions to our town was not surprising as we weren't on any map and were way out in the middle of nowhere. What was surprising was that he wanted to go there. No one ever wanted to visit our town, or not that I could ever recall. The potatoes we harvested that held no magic were taken by the elders in huge lorries to towns that took days to reach to prevent outsiders from visiting.

And those trips were only for senior members of the town. No matter how many times the younger Fingerlings asked to ride along, we were all denied. There was a good reason for that, or so the elders said if I listened to them, which I often didn't. Why would I? They were always full of doom and gloom about what could happen to a Fingerling if anyone figured out what we were. Potato shifters, from all accounts, were a strange phenomenon.

When I'd come to understand my strangeness, I'd gone in search of answers. The elders were clueless as to why the universe had decided the world required potatoes to shift. Clearly, it was strange when we didn't appear to have any purpose. I mean, were we intended as a meal to be consumed by other shifters? Nah, that couldn't be all we'd been created for, right? Well, I hoped not. Although, I'd let my mate eat me if he wanted to. I could regenerate myself if he left about a third of me. It was one of my special qualities, along with shifting fully clothed, which had always seemed like a useless gift when everyone else around me was naked when they shifted. Today had proved that it could be of benefit...*if your wolf hadn't rejected you.*

Let it drop. I argued with myself, letting the dirt coat me in the hopes its rare qualities would ease my pain. No one could explain what it was about the earth that created life and gave Fingerlings different elements of magic. One of my brothers could dig the earth with his thoughts. It was cool to watch how he could create a ten-foot wall of earth in seconds. I'd been envious until I'd been mangled in one of the large machines used to harvest the fields and discovered I could regenerate.

Everyone in their potato form could see and feel, but the elders of the town were the only ones who could communicate with all the Fingerlings in their potato form. Me, I could only do that with my siblings, which was the norm for families, which could grow to enormous numbers. I had twenty brothers. The town's population was over ten thousand. There were always new houses popping up everywhere to accommodate the growing families.

The earlier scent of Christmas and roasted spiced nuts, which I loved this time of year, increased as I neared the outskirts of town. With a thought, I stood fully dressed on the side of the dirt road, scanning the surrounding buildings. The streets were empty and my brows arched up as I realized which house the truck was stopped at. Jem's house, the oldest non-elder Fingerling. Many say that was because he was ornery and tended to poopoo all that the elders said at town meetings. I often went just to watch Jem throw out his comments like sharp barbs at those stupid enough to argue with him.

Had he invited the wolf here?

Since there was no one close by, I didn't need to worry too much about keeping out of view, so I darted around the back of a row of houses to Jem's workshop. He had several classic cars that he tinkered with and, from time to time, he'd sell one and then buy another to fix up.

Was that what the wolf was here for?

When I heard the deep, growly voice coming from the open window at the back of Jem's, I inched closer. "This transmission looks as good as new."

"Of course it does. I fixed it. I told you it was as good as the day it was made," Jem muttered, sounding annoyed like usual.

"Not everyone tells the truth."

There was an undignified snort. "Listen here, I don't tell lies, and I don't take to havin' my honor questioned by others, boy."

"I'm no boy, and I'm just sayin' as it is," the wolf growled back. His features formed into a deep scowl as he stared at Jem.

"You want that transmission or dontcha?"

The wolf relaxed a little as he examined the transmission once more. "I didn't drive all this way for nothin'."

"Then let's go up to the house and talk about the price." Jem came toward the door, which was by the window I was peeking in. He gave me a sly wink.

My eyes widened before I darted back, my heart jackrabbiting. How did he know I was there?

I changed back into my potato form and dropped to the ground as the door opened.

"This place, it's kinda weird," the wolf said as he walked past me, his nose wrinkling as he looked about as if searching for something. "You smell that?"

"Smell what?" Jem asked as he bent and picked me up.

I wriggled in his hand in fright. What was the old shifter up to?

His fingers stroked over my skin as if to reassure me everything was going to be all right, but I couldn't figure out how. The wolf continued to sniff the air, his dark brows merging together in one straight line as he eyed Jem's hand suspiciously.

Chapter Three

Tala

In the drive into Potatoville, I'd shaken off the stupid notion that—whatever that thing was—was my mate. Now that damn smell was back again, and my wolf was yipping and dancing in my head, back to driving me nuts with his excitement.

"Forget it," I muttered, not taking my eyes off the potato the shifter in front of me had just picked up off the ground.

Had the thing wriggled in his hand?

Fuck, this place was messing with my head. First, the little dude on the side of the road kept appearing and disappearing. I'd tried to figure if I'd seen a small animal on the ground or a bug in the air, anything that would explain what he was. My vision was excellent, and all I'd seen were potatoes in the damn fields.

I was starting to think I'd been taken into a fucking episode of *The Twilight Zone*. The shifter in front of me I couldn't identify and, though I was a grumpy fucker, I was never rude, or not intentionally. All right, I could be, but asking another shifter what he was could be perceived as an insult. And as I wanted the transmission now I'd seen it, I wasn't up for offending him with that question and having to leave without it.

When the dude continued to stay in the same spot stroking the potato, the weirdness factor increased.

"We gonna do this?" I wanted to get the hell out of there.

Jem held out his hand, holding the large potato, offering it to me. His eyes gleamed with something that set off tiny alarm bells, but I couldn't focus, not when my wolf went wild. Without a thought, I held out my hand. The second the potato touched my skin, electricity shot through my body. I jerked, and my fingers wrapped protectively around the potato. Instantly, my wolf settled, making contented noises I'd never heard it make before.

"I figured right," Jem said, making no sense at all.

With effort, I looked from the potato that felt extremely warm in my hand to Jem. "Whatcha talkin' 'bout?"

"That Fingerling, Tala. It's yours."

My brows shot up my forehead. "Say what?" This was turning into the weirdest day of my life.

Jem chuckled. "Don't worry. Frenchie isn't annoying. Not like some of the others."

What the fuck?

The dude had clearly lost his marbles somewhere along the way.

For want of doing anything else, I put the potato in the pocket of my jeans. My cock took instant notice while my wolf was back to lying on his back, panting. I blew out a breath. Maybe I was coming down with wolf fever?

"There's nothin' wrong with you," Jem nodded at me. "Some things are just harder to explain than others. You'll be okay. Now let's go and talk money."

The whole situation felt surreal. I sat with a hard-on that wouldn't quit, no matter what I thought about. The shifter looked so damn pleased that I got the sense I'd missed something when, an hour later, I drove off with a sack of what appeared to be more dirt than potatoes and the transmission in the back of my truck. The potato Jem had handed to me remained in my pocket. I couldn't make myself take it out. And with all the weirdness, I decided just to leave and not think too hard about it.

On the drive back, I spent hours trying to work out what was wrong with me. I felt out of sorts like I'd never experienced before. Hot and bothered with this odd feeling in the center of my chest. By the time I finally got back to town, I'd convinced myself that I was coming down with something nasty. As it was late and the town doc didn't like visitors unless someone was dying, I chose to leave him alone and headed straight to the auto shop. It was the middle of the night as I parked, and the place was in darkness. I was the only one stupid enough to work late at night. I had nothing else to do with my time, and it meant I got more done without others hanging around bothering me.

The potato moved in my pocket as I got out of the truck. I glanced down, waited for a beat, and shook my head.

I was delirious. I had to be. There was no way a potato could move on its own. I was definitely heading straight for Doc's in the morning. I went and unlocked the side entrance to the shop, shutting out the worry for now, or at least I was going to try.

Returning to the truck, I took the transmission out of the cab and carried it inside. My cock pressed uncomfortably against my jeans as I bent to place the transmission on the low shelf I'd made space on the day before. I cursed at the arousal that pulsed and fought with the button fly of my jeans. I stood and thumped at my cock, hoping that would give me a damn break.

When nothing happened, I glanced down warily. This was too much. Maybe I needed to get laid? Maybe that was what was wrong with me. It had been a while since I'd used anything but my hand. The thought got my wolf growling and pacing in my mind. "What the fuck is wrong with you?"

It snarled and pushed for dominance. Something it never did.

Recalling how I'd felt, standing on the dirt in Potatoville, a shiver ran through me. *Has the strange earth done something to me? To my wolf?*

I wasn't normally one to give in to silly notions, but this one wouldn't budge as I locked up the auto shop and got back in the truck. Between my cock and my wolf, by the time I pulled up outside my cabin, I was ready for a cold beer and...I wasn't sure what else with how anxious my wolf was.

Inside my cabin, I switched on the lights. The room glowed warmly, and there was a feeling of peacefulness to the place. I'd built the cabin, and though it was rustic in appearance, it had all the modern conventions a wolf could want. The polished wooden walls gleamed under the spotlights as I bypassed the large sofa that sat in front of my seventy-five-inch TV. The ground-floor space was all open with large windows front and back to allow the light in and let me see the forest surrounding my home. In the daylight, when the sun hit them just right, the trees cast green shadows throughout my home and gave the illusion I was in the forest. My wolf loved to lie in front of the open window, snoozing, enjoying the warm air and scents of the wood.

The living room flowed into the kitchen, and I headed straight for the refrigerator to grab a beer. Top off, I drank deep, hoping it would somehow rid me of the unsettled feeling that hadn't let go since my brief encounter with...whatever he was.

Holding the bottle in my hand, I stared at the countertop where a covered plate lay. Clearly, my brother had asked one of the omega's to make me a meal. I rubbed at my stomach, and my little finger brushed over the potato that, for some bizarre reason, I'd kept in my pocket throughout the trip home.

I pushed my hand inside my jeans, and the possessive feelings I'd had when Jem had placed the thing in my hand returned. Jeez, this was too fucking much. I stared intently at the potato. "What is it about you that is making me so damn crazy?" I laughed at my own ridiculousness when my voice echoed in the room.

The laughter got stuck in my throat as the potato rolled out of my hand, and a second later, the tiny man I'd seen on the dirt road appeared. The bottle slipped out of my hand and crashed to the floor.

The tiny man jumped back and tutted. "Be careful. I don't want a load of glass in my skin. In human form, it takes longer to regenerate when I don't have the dirt to use."

The same strange sing-song voice said that I wasn't imagining this, that I was indeed in my kitchen with the man from the roadside.

This is impossible.

There was no such thing as a...
"What...no...fuck...what...Christ..."

I stepped to the side, glass crunching under my boots. I ran a shaky hand over my face and shut my eyes. *This isn't real. This isn't real.*

I was seriously ill, hallucinating about a potato shifting. That was it. I was going to see the doc. Now. There was no way I could wait till morning.

I opened my eyes and met those of...
For fuck's sake!
My mate!

Chapter Four

Frenchie

The panic at Jem offering me to the wolf had lasted until the shifter had wrapped his fingers around my skin. The warmth and scent of him were hard to resist, especially when it tempted me to shift. I'd resisted, just, and boy did that bring a huge benefit when he'd slipped me into his pocket. The scent of his arousal was yummy and dirty thoughts had filled my mind, keeping me occupied for nearly all the trip.

I'd thought about why Jem had decided to give me to the shifter, but it was hard to focus with the warmth and feel of his body pressed against mine. Yeah, who needed to figure that out when I was with my mate. Only he'd yet again gone and spoiled my daydreaming that the next time he saw me, he'd be happier. The way he moved away and wore a disbelieving expression crushed my already tender heart.

I was a decent shifter. I was! There'd be many happy to be mated to me, I was sure of it.

As I gave myself a talking too, I stood taller and inhaled a deep breath, then wished I hadn't when my body reacted painfully. My temper started to fizzle. "What? Don't you want your mate?"

"You're not my mate." Even as he said it, his animal appeared in his eyes.

My pulse skidded to a halt for several beats as the man shifted into his animal form. There was the sound of tearing clothes and bones popping as his large body morphed into a huge black wolf. It stood nearly as tall as me, its powerful body rippling with fur and muscles. His large jaw was full of sharp teeth that looked as if they could rip a man's head clear off.

Its eyes glittered with...*hunger*.

I gulped. "Nice wolfy," I muttered in fright, then rolled my eyes, much like the wolf did, at how ridiculous that sounded. A flush of heat rode up my neck, and I dipped my gaze. "Sorry about that. It was a stupid thing to say. You just gave me a little fright, that's all. I thought you were rejecting me. Are you?"

The last bit came out more like a squeak when the wolf growled low and stepped closer. His nose lifted. The next growl was more...well, I couldn't say what it was as I'd never met a wolf before, but I liked it. My body definitely liked it, judging by how it was reacting.

The nose was in my groin before I could figure that was what the wolf intended to do, although if I were honest, I don't think I would have moved out of reach even if I had. A large tongue licked over the fabric of my shorts, and I shivered. Painful arousal like I'd never experienced before had my knees locking out to stop them from shaking. My cock leaked, and the scent of my arousal mixed with that of the wolf. He made an odd noise then repeated the action once more as I panted through the need to come in my pants.

My hips canted forward of their own accord, seeking more. I ran a hand over the soft-looking fur, which was silky under my palm. He made a kind of happy sound. Or that's what I thought it was, but it was hard to concentrate when his nose was pressed against my throbbing cock. I sucked in another breath, fighting the urges to strip and bare my slick-feeling ass. It was all so confusing.

"I'm Frenchie, by the way. You didn't ask, but that's my name. I heard Jem call you Tala. It's nice to meet you." I panted past the next wave of arousal. "Maybe we should take some time and get to know each other. You know, before we get to the sex part? I've never had sex, and I'm not sure how that's going to work. Do you do it in your wolf form?"

There was a strangled noise before the wolf became a man. An exceptionally large, very naked man. The hair I'd imagined covered a massive chest and led down his happy trail to the thick arousal bobbing between us. I swallowed in an attempt to wet my mouth as my gaze lingered on his huge, aroused cock, which looked angry with the mushroom head red and slick, a drop of precum suspended from the tip.

It appeared to be offering me a gift in a kind of greeting I was more than happy to accept. There were weird sensations in my ass, and the slick I'd noticed earlier started to drip from my body.

The man's nose wrinkled, and the hunger I'd seen in the wolf's eyes was there in the man's as his teeth bared. "Mine," he growled.

Oh, dear!

There was no time to react as I was lifted bodily off the floor and flung over the guy's shoulder. The air left my body, my lungs struggling to take in the next breath while my cock tried to drill a hole in the guy's chest.

"Talk, don't you think? Talking is good," I said nervously, even though that was the last thing on my mind. My body wanted this, whether or not my head was still trying to figure out the logistics of that cock fitting in my ass. All the talk on mates had never involved the sex part. Why was that?

I landed on a huge bed and bounced twice. As the situation finally sank in about what was about to happen I shifted, in full panic mode.

There was an angry growl as I was lifted off the mattress in the palm of the guy's hand. "This has to be some fucking almighty joke. There is no such thing as a potato shifter. There just isn't. I'm hallucinating. This whole thing is not fucking real. I need to see the doc!"

There was hurt at his words, but I got it. I'd struggled to understand why we were what we were. How was my mate supposed to understand it when he hadn't known I existed until now? I sighed and shifted back. He immediately dropped me on the bed, which I was grateful for because it was soft under my ass.

Back to stepping away from me, I tried not to take offense. "Listen, I get it. I do. It's hard to comprehend that potatoes can shift, but we're as real as you. You're not hallucinating." I left off the part about being his mate when he didn't appear all that happy about what I was.

His hand lifted then dropped back to his side. "You're a…potato shifter?"

"I am. So is Jem. The whole town, all of us are."

That seemed to unbalance him as he staggered to the bed and sat down next to me, once more making it hard to focus with his arousal right there.

"Do you think you could put some clothes on…it's really hard to concentrate with…" I eyed his groin hungrily.

He got up wordlessly and went to the closet. Two minutes later, he wore a T-shirt and a pair of briefs that hardly contained his cock, not that I was paying that much attention, I wasn't. I mean, it was right there. It wasn't as if I was staring.

Oh god, I was staring.

"If you want to talk, then talk. After that, I'm taking you back to fuck-ville."

Chapter Five

Tala

I stared at the screen of my computer and tried to block out the noise coming from the other side of the kitchen. I wasn't sure how I'd been persuaded to let the dude stay. My wolf growled low and mean, and it wasn't at the man making us breakfast.

"Does Jem have a phone?" I asked grudgingly when I couldn't find the number in any of the correspondence I'd had with him. There was an extensive list of stuff I needed to do, and getting rid of Frenchie was top of it. After his explanation about what he was, I'd been exhausted and a little disbelieving, even when he'd shown me what he was capable of.

I'd left him in the spare room, too tired to force myself to drive back to his hometown. Or that's what I was trying to make myself believe. My wolf wasn't letting me off the hook so easily and had made sure I got fuck-all for sleep. How was I meant to sleep when the scent in the house left my wolf and me hungry and horny?

"He does." Frenchie sucked his lower lip between his teeth and his brow scrunched up, then a second later, he recited a number.

Grabbing my cell phone, I typed in the number and waited for it to be answered. I tapped my fingers on the table several times before a voice came through the speaker.

"Who is this, and where'd you get my number?"

A smile tugged at my lips at how the dude sounded much like me, grumpy. "It's Tala. I'm the guy who bought the transmission yesterday. You gave me..." I met Frenchie's sad eyes. "A potato."

"And."

"I don't want it."

There was a choked sob before Frenchie fled from the room, and the sound of bare feet hitting the wooden stairs followed. My wolf snarled, desperate to follow. When I resisted, it started to howl, and I hunched in the chair, rubbing at my head, trying to concentrate.

"What do you mean you don't want it? You can't give it back. He's yours now."

The fact the old-timer called the potato *he* told me he knew exactly what I was talking about, which got my anger going from simmering, where it had been since the damn potato had shifted into...

Nope, I wasn't going there. My anger, as far as I was concerned, was justified. There was no way an alpha wolf would be mated to a potato. Nope, not in my lifetime was that ever happening. "No, old man, he is not mine."

There was a disgruntled sigh. "Why do distinct species believe they're better than others? See, this is why we don't reveal our existence. Dicks like you. He's your mate, you know this, your wolf knows this, Frenchie knows this. The moment you drove off with him, he became yours. He can't return here. Magic doesn't allow it. If you don't want him, then he's going to have to make it on his own." With that, the phone went dead, and my already fast-beating heart went crazy.

I slammed the phone down on the table, the cracking sound that came after hardly registering past the warring emotions and my animal howling inside my head. The idea of Frenchie out in the world alone was too much. I stomped to the door leading into the forest behind my home, my wolf taking full control. I barely had time to strip before my muscles contorted and I leaped off the wooden veranda, landing with four feet on the soft grass. My wolf threw back its head and howled long and loud. The cries would alert my brother and the other pack mates of the distress. For my wolf, it was clear-cut. Stop fucking about and claim our mate.

It wasn't so clear-cut.

What did a wolf shifter do with a potato, for god's sake, besides eat it? It wasn't as if I'd ever thought about being mated. That was what others wanted. I just wanted to be left alone to get on with my life.

Once more, my wolf was not in agreement.

How the fuck does a potato give birth to pups? You're being fucking ridiculous.

The next howl was full of disagreement as we took off into the forest. Animals fled as if sensing the distress of my wolf. Wolf firmly in control, it headed where it wanted, running as if the devil was chasing. The hope inside my wolf was that with a little time to think about my behavior, I'd come to my senses and see that what the fates had given us was a gift.

The familiar scents that normally helped to calm us both did nothing with the fury aimed at me for what it perceived was my lack of good judgment. At the sound of another wolf approaching, I lifted my large head and scented my brother. Seconds later, he appeared from the large group of trees that led from the boundary of my home. His eyes were full of concern as he came around me to run at my side, his wolf rubbing against mine. His alpha presence didn't work on me, but my wolf calmed a little.

What is wrong, brother? You've got the whole pack antsy.

It's none of your business.

Don't give me that shit.

I didn't bother to respond. Instead, I increased my pace. The trees thickened and the large canopy overhead shut out the light. The scent of wet earth and foliage increased. There was a green hue cast over everything around us. It gave the place an ethereal glow. Deafening water crashed against a rock when we came to a stop by the side of the massive waterfall that sat slap bang in the middle of my land. My wolf dove straight into the freshwater without pause.

I cursed, air stuck in my chest at the fresh iciness, then moaned in delight with my wolf. There was something freeing about being in the water.

There was a splash next to me, and I surfaced with my brother, droplets of water glistening off his fur. *Talk to me.*

Can't you just leave it be for once?

No. You handed over the role of alpha to me. That means I can't. You know damn well I can feel your pain, your wolf's pain.

Hey now, I'm not in pain.

Whatever. If your wolf is hurting, then so are you.

If it was possible, I was sure he rolled his eyes at me before he swam to the edge of the pool and leaped out, shaking the water from his fur. He lay down on the small crop of rocks where the sun penetrated the canopy.

You're gonna wait, aren't you?

Yep. The answer was followed by him shutting his eyes and resting his large head on his front paws. His fur was several shades lighter than mine and gleamed with vitality in the sun.

I turned away and swam toward the waterfall and let it beat against my head. The power of the water always felt cathartic as it pounded against my skull. Today all it did was irritate me. This was all my brother's fault.

I eyed the wolf on the rocks and growled.

I can hear your thoughts. And what's my fault?

I swam back to him, and since I wasn't going to get any peace, I got out of the water and shook right next to him, covering him in droplets of water.

Childish much? He stood and shook his fur once more before the animal turned to man. There was deep concern in his eyes, and I hated that I'd put it there. "Talk to me."

My animal relinquished its hold at the alpha demand. I stood as naked as my twin. The two of us were hard to tell apart other than the color of his hair, which matched the coat of his fur, and if anyone looked closely, they'd see he was an inch or two shorter. Keeping my voice lowered as I was always the cautious one, I muttered, "I've found my mate."

Olowin's smile was instant. "Brother, congratulations on your mating." His eyes traveled over my skin and his brow furrowed, though he continued to radiate happiness.

"We're not mated, and I have no intention of mating with him." I ground out. My wolf was back to howling, and Olowin was looking as if I'd lost the plot.

Could a potato mark his mate? I shivered with desire, then closed off the ideas my brain and wolf gave me.

He scratched at his bristly jaw, his eyes narrowing. "Why not? What's wrong with him? Is he another alpha?"

I snorted and dejectedly sat down on a rock, watching the water spray. "If that was the fucking issue. I never wanted a mate and not a…" I couldn't bring myself to say it.

Olowin sat down next to me and dangled his feet in the water, unconcerned about the iciness lapping at his calves. "What is he? Is that the problem? Is he not a wolf? Something else? A cat? A bear? An eagle? It doesn't matter what he is. The pack will accept him."

I blew out a breath and met my brother's stare. The list he'd reeled off, I think I could have coped with, maybe. "A…pot…ta…to."

He blinked, then coughed, then snorted before he started to laugh. He slapped at my shoulder hard enough to fell a tree.

I growled in warning.

"It's not like you to be the joker," he said through raucous laughter.

I held his gaze until it registered that I wasn't joking. It took another two minutes before he stopped laughing and for the smile to disappear from his face. "No…seriously…there's no such thing as a potato shifter…is there?" The disbelief matched my own.

Out of the corner of my eye, I caught some movement. A brown ball rolled to the base of the rock where we were sitting, and my heart picked up speed at the scent of crispy fries and rich ketchup. My body reacted, as did my wolf, before Frenchie appeared a second later.

I didn't acknowledge the part of me that was pleased he was fully clothed in front of my brother. That, I'd have to think about later.

There was a big splash, and my brother surfaced a moment later, spluttering. He wiped at his eyes, his gaze on the man standing looking down at him, offering a shy smile.

"Hi, I'm Frenchie."

"Holy fuck!" Olowin gasped, his eyes alight with curiosity. "You're a..."

"Potato shifter, yes. But I've always been told not to talk about it with strangers. Does it count when I've never actually met a stranger until you? Not that you're strange. You look like a nice shifter. One that isn't going to do horrible things to me." Frenchie's smile warmed and a worm of jealousy, something I'd never thought myself capable of, grew when he didn't so much as look in my direction.

The amusement at Olowin falling off the rock into the water waned. My brother heaved himself back onto the ground and, as he'd done in his animal form, shook his body. His body was as large and powerful as mine and equally as naked.

Frenchie's eyes widened as they traveled over my brother's body. "Wow! You look exactly the same as Tala. Even your—"

I got up and stood in front of Frenchie, cutting off his view. "We're twins."

He tilted his head back to look at me. There was nothing but sadness in his eyes. Not the joy or mischief I'd seen a moment ago. "Twins, that explains it."

A sudden panicky feeling rose that I didn't like in the slightest. "Explain what?" I barked out.

His brows arched. "Why you look very similar, even down to the size of your—"

Heat rode up my neck and my cock bobbed when his gaze lowered. "Shoe size, yes. We're identical," I said, cutting him off once more.

The little nose wrinkle was adorable.

No, it isn't.

"You're not identical. The hair coloring is different. You have more lines around your mouth and eyes. His are less, which I'd say is because he's maybe not as grumpy as you." He moved to peek around my shoulder. "He's not as tall as you either, I don't think."

His observations were spot on, but I didn't reply since I was starting to worry about whether or not our mating could be different from others, and maybe Frenchie...

He's cute.

He's mine.

You said you didn't want him.

Fuck off.

"Why are you scowling like that? Your wolf wanted me to follow. I was only doing what it

47

wanted. Is that wrong?" His shaggy hair swayed as he shook his head. "The town elders, I think, messed things up. It's either that or they aren't up-to-date with all things to do with matings. No one told me I could be rejected. I'm sorry you got stuck with me."

"Jeez." I scowled. My wolf demanded I fix things and remove the sad expression from Frenchie's face. "It's not that I don't want you…" The moment the words left my lips before my brain could engage, I knew I was in trouble.

His eyes brightened, then my arms were full as Frenchie launched himself at me, climbing me like a monkey climbing a damn tree. Next thing I knew, he was peppering kisses all over my face. His scent increased, and for the life of me, I couldn't get my arms to release him as he clung on.

There was laughter in my head. *I'll leave you to it, and we can talk about…whatever he is later. Congratulations, brother, on finding your mate.*

I could barely concentrate on anything other than the man rubbing himself all over me, or that's what it felt like. His lips were soft as they roamed freely over my face. Small hands ran through the hair on my chest, and he made little delighted sounds. The scent of dirt that lingered around him decreased with the scent of his arousal.

My wolf surged forward, desperate to bite, to claim our mate. Shudders wracked my body as I struggled not to give in to the baser urges. His nose brushed against mine when his hands cupped my cheeks gently. The touch gave me a similar feeling to the one I'd had when I got out of the truck the first time I encountered him. This time it was much stronger, and serenity flowed through me as my anxiety fled.

Eyes that had once appeared pale were now ocean-blue and full of desire. "I'll behave and be the best mate you ever could want. Although being good can be hard for me. My family is always telling me off for being too inquisitive. It's how we met. I did promise myself to remain in my potato form, then I scented you and well…" He sighed, laid his head on my chest, and snuggled in. "I'll try my best to be what you want."

Fucked! I was so fucked at how giddy my damn wolf was.

I sighed.

It was only my wolf that wanted Frenchie…*sort of*.

Chapter Six

Frenchie

After Tala had rejected me once again, I ran upstairs to the bedroom, but moments later, there'd been a distinct pull inside me, encouraging me back out. I knew it was his wolf spirit calling to me. I couldn't explain it. I just knew it wanted me. Since I was feeling a little hurt by the rejection, I'd resisted...*yeah, for all of five minutes!*

I rolled my eyes heavenward and snuggled closer to Tala, who thankfully didn't seem inclined to put me down. Although his muscles *were* tense. Was that from holding me?

I mentally slapped my own forehead when it was clear that the wolf was having no problem carrying me. Time passed, and I wasn't sure how long it was after Tala's brother disappeared before Tala walked back to the rock he'd been sitting on. His thighs bunched under my ass as he positioned me with care, so I didn't impale myself on his monster dick. The slick feeling in my ass increased, and I was positive he could scent exactly what effect he was having on me if I wasn't leaving a damp patch on his skin.

When he did nothing more and remained silent, I started to ramble. It was a habit I had when I was nervous. "I'm a hard worker, and I know I'm small, but I'm stronger than I look..." The hands that were resting at the base of my back let go and moved under my arms. Taking hold, they eased me back so I could see his expression. I groaned at the hint of fang and the intensity of the eyes staring at me, which were mostly animal.

Fuck!

My words dried up.

The intoxicating scent of Christmas coming off him increased, and his dick pulsed against the front of my T-shirt. The sounds of the water cascading down the rocks and into the pool behind me prevented him from hearing me puffing like the train I'd once heard. To distract myself, I glanced away, desperately unsure about what came next. He'd rejected me and, regardless of how my body wasn't keeping any secrets on how much I wanted him, he was conflicted.

This place was hidden deep in the forest, and I could see why he'd come here. It was peaceful and beautiful. And though I wasn't sure he'd want me to say it, it was romantic. Maybe his wolf was wooing me. A warmth grew past the hurt as that thought took root.

"We need to...talk about this situation."

My heart started to pound. "All right." The nerves were there in my voice, and there was nothing I could do to stop them. Was he going to reject me again?

My hands tightened on his shoulders, my eyes begging.

"Fuck, why you gotta look at me like that?" He growled, and suddenly his lips were on mine, stopping the next barrage of rambling.

His lips were firm, and the taste was the same as his scent. God, I wanted to gobble him up. My lips parted, and I let him do as he wished. If that made me a desperate hoe, who cared?

Bold kisses turned deeper as his tongue stroked over my lips before delving into my mouth to taste me. His tongue slid over mine, and I felt the touch in places I never expected. My toes curled and my ass was back to feeling weird. I ground my pelvis against his dick and groaned when his hands slipped to my ass and firmly kneaded the muscles.

"Naked," he muttered against my mouth.

"You are?" My brow wrinkled, and I tugged back to look down at his body.

His eyes glittered. "You. You need to be naked."

I swallowed hard at what would happen when I was. "Oh. I thought you wanted to talk first? Or was that me?"

"Fuck talking!"

I could get on board with that. I wanted this. I did. I'd dreamed of it. Not so much it happening outside where others could watch. No, that's not quite what I'd envisioned with my mate. I sensed there was no one near, but before I could reach for the edges of my top, it was in two pieces on the ground. I blinked at the wolf's claw, then my shorts met the same fate.

My mouth hung open. Panic flared at the unknown. "What am I going to do now? They're the only clothes I have. Will they regenerate when I shift? I've never had to think about that."

"You talk too much," he muttered. There was no time to reply or take offense as his mouth touched mine in another hungry kiss.

This one was all about heat and passion, melting me into a pile of goo. Or that's what it felt like as I draped over Tala's chest. The heat of his body penetrated mine as his body hair brushed enticingly over my skin.

With his mouth back on mine, my thoughts rolled into each other, and I couldn't focus on any of them with so many sensations bombarding me. I gave up trying and ran my hands over his broad shoulder muscles that rippled under my touch, then down his back as far as I could reach, flattening my chest to his. His body was glorious. When potatoes were in human form, they were wirier and tended to be short. The thought I'd had previously about rolling over his body was there, clinging on. My cock thickened, and slick dripped from my ass.

His chest moved quickly as his hands slipped over my smooth skin, leaving shivers of desire in their wake. They spread everywhere. The kiss was distracting as he sucked on my tongue, and I undulated against him.

Hard! His body was so damn firm. The hair made for a stark contradiction with how soft it was.

Large hands slid over my ass, and I started to gasp into his mouth. Lips trailed over my cheek to my ear, his tongue licking down the side of my neck until it met the junction of my throat and shoulder.

"Smell so good." His nose buried in the crook, and he moaned, sending yet more shivers of desire through me.

God, how could it be this good, and he hadn't touched my dick?

As if he could read me, his fingers traced down the seam of my ass. Normally, I'd have been mortified about how wet I was for him, but he short-circuited my brain with the finger, using my slick to tease the sensitive skin.

"Ooh," I cried out as he twirled his finger repeatedly over my hole. Tiny fires lit up my ass, and it clenched, desperate for more. I clung to his broad shoulders and prayed he would never stop.

His teeth grazed the skin of my neck, and I arched back, giving him access to the column of my throat.

"So beautiful," he growled, low and deep. His hot breath brushed over the skin, and shudders made it difficult for me to keep seated on his legs.

The finger playing with my ass and his mouth on my body were...heaven. "More," I cried when his finger continued to tease the outer rim. My body was made for him. I had to believe that, even with the little thread of fear deep inside that he was too big for my small body.

The tip of his finger easily breached my ass, and the weird sensations from earlier started to make sense as my sphincter relaxed and pleasure followed without pain. "Ooh...that's what it means."

Hungry eyes met mine, his brows merging as he shook his head. "What? What are you talking about now?"

I grinned at how grumpy he was. "My ass. It felt funny. Not bad funny, just a little weird. I think it's because it knows you're my mate, so it's happy. You know, it's opening, so you don't hurt me. You're so big, and I was worried you wouldn't fit."

He groaned, and before I could fret that I'd gone too far with the rambling again, his head tipped back and he started to laugh. It was deep and infectious. I grinned at him. I gave in to the temptation to run my hands through the fur on his chest. "Can I roll over your chest?"

The laughter became choked, and his eyes widened. "What?"

I blushed. The heat persisted as he stared at me with an expression I couldn't read. "I had this image when we first met of rolling over your body...in my potato form."

His arousal pulsed against me, and the precum coming from his cock slicked my stomach. That had to be a good thing, right? I examined his face closely. His nostrils were flared. Were his fangs longer?

"I…yes." He glanced away, and when his gaze returned to me, he scowled. "Change, and I'll carry you back to the house in my mouth."

I squealed. "Really? How fun will that be!" Off his lap before he could change his mind, I shifted. He caught me before I could hit the ground. A warmth I was starting to love grew in my chest at how he stared at me intently before placing me on the rock and shifting into his wolf.

Ooh!

The big teeth and huge mouth seemed even larger as the wolf approached, sniffed the air above me, then scooped me up into his mouth. I rested against his tongue, and my mind was back to having thoughts I was sure would send me to hell.

Chapter Seven

Tala

Madness, it was all madness.

How could I get aroused from the idea of Frenchie's potato rolling over my body? It was absurd. That didn't seem to make any difference to my dick, which was leaking like a broken tap all over the damn place, showing it was more than happy for the madness.

In my wolf form, I stared at the potato, which sat wriggling on the rock with apparent excitement at what was coming next. Opening wide, I gently used my tongue to roll the potato into my mouth, careful to keep him from my sharp incisors. Although I tasted a little dirt, which I had been expecting, I was surprised to find all that remained was Frenchie's sweetness.

Overloaded with my wolf's constant thoughts on what should happen the moment we got back to the house, it was hard not to let him take charge. I acknowledged for the first time in the last twenty-four hours that maybe my wolf was right. It yipped, and Frenchie rubbed himself against my tongue, and what my soul had already known, the rightness of this—whatever this was—spread through me.

There was no more fighting it, and I wasn't certain if that was because I was in my wolf form or that the potato had started to grow on me. Even thinking about it, the strangeness didn't take away from the situation.

The weight of him in my mouth was barely noticeable as I ran through the forest, the sounds and smells that enticed me to linger the last things on my mind. Bounding into the house through the open doors, I headed straight to the bedroom with a wiggling potato hitting my teeth as I came to a halt at the side of the bed. I opened my jaw and lowered my head toward the mattress, letting him plop onto the cover.

A second later, the potato became a man and my wolf receded so I could shift. I stared at a naked Frenchie.

His gaze was lowered to his body and a panicked expression appeared. "Oh no, my clothes! You need to go back and get them," he squealed.

That was not what I was going to do, hell no. I'd resisted the little imp for long enough, and clothes were not what we were going to be needing any time soon. My wolf was in full agreement.

"You won't be needin' them." My gaze traveled the length of him. He might have been small, but he was beautifully proportioned. His limbs were slender with lean muscles, and his skin was golden if not a little streaked with bits of dirt. He was completely hairless, which I got. No one wanted a hairy potato. The weirdness of that was pushed aside as I lowered one knee onto the bed.

Frenchie finally met my stare, his brows arching up. "Ever again?" he asked, giving me a cheeky smile that brought dimples to his cheeks.

I swallowed and worked to keep my wolf in check when all he wanted to do was pounce and bite the delectable man.

"You ain't wanderin' around here naked with the pack so close by," I growled.

"I like that possessive tone," he shivered, his cock jerking in his lap as if in agreement.

My wolf was all but doing a damn happy dance at the declaration, and I bit back the retort that I'd have normally let fly without thought. "We'll see," I muttered instead and decided talking was overrated.

Lifting myself fully onto the bed, the mattress dipped, and Frenchie, instead of rolling closer to me, edged back toward the large wooden headboard.

A smile that was all wolf spread over my lips. "Now, where do you think you're goin'?"

He bit his lower lip and his blond eyelashes lowered. For the first time, he didn't seem to have anything to say. I crawled up the bed and over his outstretched legs until I caged him in.

"I'm grumpy, I don't have a nice disposition, I shout a lot, and I like being alone." He released his lip, but other than it quivering, he remained silent. "It would seem I'm also a possessive bastard who doesn't like the idea of anyone seeing you like this. It ain't supposed to be like this, but fuck if I want to change it."

My gaze swept over him once more, this time in acceptance of what I'd known deep down when I'd first seen him. The universe and the pack be damned.

His eyes sparkled, and I huffed out a put-upon breath.

"It's okay. I'm used to grumpy folks, and I've learned to shout back. No one has ever been possessive of me. I think I might like that."

He looked too damn pleased that I just gave in, and I threw back my head laughing. "You're gonna be trouble."

His answering grin was all mischief.

I shook my head and ignored the niggle of worry that I'd taken on more than I could handle, given how easily he could make me behave differently. His delicateness stopped me from dropping all my weight onto him as I came forward to kiss him. His mouth called to me with full lips that begged to be kissed.

His lower lip was swollen from where he'd bitten it. I licked over the pink flesh, and he moaned, his eyelids fluttering closed. His breath came in small bursts over my face as I repeated the action, gaining a shiver. The driving urge to bite and fuck was held with iron control as I simply enjoyed the flavor of *my mate*. He was mine!

Why had I not wanted this?

The answer wasn't important as I deepened the kiss degree by degree, sinking into the dreamy sounds he was making. The few times I'd bothered with other wolves for sex, it had been quick and hard. There'd been no foreplay, no kissing. They weren't things I thought I'd have enjoyed. Frenchie dispelled me of that notion as his lips parted and his small hands came up to touch my chest as he had done earlier. Fingertips lightly ran over the hair, then a little firmer as he moaned and hands started to roam freely. Suddenly, I was the one groaning.

His touch was warm and his palms rough against me. Rough calluses teased my flesh as he explored my body. Whatever thoughts or worries he'd had earlier were no longer an issue, or so I assumed, given how he was pushing up toward me as if he was trying to rub against every part of me. Our dicks connected, and we groaned in unison as precum allowed them to glide against each other in a sensual slide.

The scent of his musk increased, and my teeth dropped with my wolf wanting to bite. His tongue licked at them, and I was panting at the intense desire flooding through me. It didn't seem to matter what he did. Each touch and sound he made amplified the feelings inside me.

With his lips chasing mine, there was a warm satisfaction I'd never felt before. I moved to lick the palm of my hand, his eyes widening as he followed the direction of it as I slipped it between us to take hold of both our cocks.

"Ooh...jeez...holyyyy...crapppp...that's....oooo oohhhh." He quivered and bucked, his skin pinking up.

I chuckled and stroked us both from base to tip, watching his eyes. His pupils became pinpoint as the blue darkened, and I found myself swimming in the ocean of them, battling wild urges. Wave after wave of pleasure rode through me as I held his gaze, stroking us both and giving us both what we wanted. The silken feel of his cock against mine was a stark contrast to what I was used to. The differences between us were never more obvious as his hands landed on the cover and his knuckles went white as he arched up into my touch. The constant stream of nonsense continued as his body undulated with each stroke of my hand. The desire for my own release wasn't important, with Frenchie displaying how elated he was to be being pleasured by me.

Each reaction plunged him a little deeper into my heart and the misgivings disappeared. "So beautiful," I rasped.

"I need...I need..."

I squeezed a little tighter and twisted my hand, bringing it back up our cocks. His head thrust back into the pillow. His body tensed, and his cock pulsed, warm cum spurting between us to coat my skin and his. The scent drove my wolf insane with the need to claim our mate. Surging forward with my own cock still painfully hard, my teeth sank into the junction between his neck and shoulder. My teeth pushed through the flesh, which was rich with the taste of him. Blood flooded my mouth as I released our cocks so I could move to spread his legs and slip sticky fingers over his taint to his ass. The groan was all inside my mind at the slick ass my finger sank into with ease. His channel convulsed around my finger and squeezed.

"Ooh...that...feels..."

The rambling stopped as I sank a second finger into his willing body. The level of desperation coming from my wolf increased with each thrust of my fingers into my mate. Frenchie started to pant, and it was all I could do to make sure he was ready. His body was made for mine, but still, I was so huge compared to him.

"In me...oh now...in me," he cried in a desperate voice that broke the chains on my control.

Teeth releasing from his neck, I licked at the bite mark, removing my fingers to replace them with my cock. Pushing against the slick rim, Frenchie groaned and tried to impale himself on my cock. I thrust into him, barely remembering the need for restraint. My cock sank deep and was clasped in slick tightness, his channel milking me for all it was worth as I struggled to breathe.

The urges, combined with Frenchie's begging, were too strong to resist, and I started to pound into him without restraint. He wailed and clung on as I let my baser instincts take over. Sounds of flesh hitting flesh hardly registered with how my body was reacting. Everything was amplified. All my senses came alive as my body shook with the violence of my cum ripping out of my cock. The pain was intense but nothing compared to the flare of life-affirming pleasure that came hot on its heels. My scent mingled with Frenchie's, his life force binding me to a tiny potato.

He shuddered and shook, his fingers digging into my shoulders. An unfamiliar sensation of heat and fire started inside my chest. It burned like wildfire, coursing its way down through my body to my cock. More cum spurted deep inside my mate as if to ensure my scent covered him inside and out while he groaned anew.

My wolf considered himself satisfied as I licked at the bite mark, which looked huge in comparison to the man who lay replete with a tiny smile on his lips. With Frenchie flushed and smelling of me, my wolf, for the moment, was content.

I slipped from his body and rolled to the side, chest heaving, to collapse on the mattress, my cock remaining hard and aroused, though I had no idea how. My eyes had barely shut when the mattress dipped and settled, alerting me that Frenchie had shifted.

Up in a panic I'd never admit to, I stared at the potato next to me. "What happened? Why have you shifted?"

There was a buzzing inside my ears, followed by a popping. I banged on my ear, never once taking my eyes off the potato. I jerked when his familiar voice filled my head.

You said you'd let me roll over you.

To gain a mind connection with a mate, I'd always been led to believe both mates had to be claimed with a bite. I blinked slowly and tried to regulate my breathing.

Can you hear me?

Frenchie's giggles came through loud and clear before he rolled to touch the side of my body. The skin of his potato was...

I left the thought there, not wanting to go down that path. It would only lead to insanity.

Of course. We've mated. He wriggled against my side. *Though you still need to...you know...let me do my thing.*

Your thing? I asked unwillingly, though I couldn't resist him when he sounded so cute and flustered. I rolled my eyes to the ceiling. *Cute? What the fuck was wrong with me?*

Why do you think it's wrong to feel I'm cute?

The hurt came through loud and clear, even before there was a sniffle and the potato rolled away from me. My wolf growled, and I didn't hunch, but it was a close call as I reached for Frenchie and picked him up.

I held the potato closer to my face, not focusing on how ridiculous I probably looked. "I'm sorry. I told you I am a grumpy fucker. I'm not gonna be able to control my thoughts, so...you have to get used to them."

He wriggled in my palm.

"What is it?"

He wriggled again.

The sigh of annoyance was long as I lay down on the bed and placed him on my chest, hoping I understood him correctly. He could talk to me, so why wasn't he? I didn't project that thought, though, as he started to roll over my body.

Whatever I'd expected from this experience, it wasn't the deep sense of calm and desire that kind of messed with my head a little. The two feelings were polar opposite, yet they fit as he rolled his way over my body.

What in damnation is he doing to me?

Chapter Eight

Frenchie

The elders had been a little vague with how the whole bonding thing happened during mating. I'd assumed they were all prudes, although it could be that they just didn't have a clue. Now that I thought about it, I wasn't sure any of them were mated to a true fated mate. Was that because they weren't accepting of other species as mates?

That wasn't something I could answer, but I wondered for the first time if Jem could. He'd been the one to bring my mate to town and had handed me over to him. How had the old potato known I was mated to Tala?

There was a contented sigh from above, and I rolled up the wolf's large chest toward his shoulder. His hooded eyes watched me as I rolled closer to his head. The heat of desire remained between us, although it no longer blazed with the same intensity. When Tala had lost control of his wolf, I'd understood then what it was like to be wanted with a passion that was unrestrained. It was heady, and my body had very much enjoyed how the wolf and man had let go.

Half-expecting there to be pain due to his sheer size and strength, there'd been only pleasure and need. The need was what had driven me to beg, and thankfully, that worked on Tala, which was a tidbit of knowledge I'd tucked away for future reference.

The silly thoughts about his preconceptions that he sometimes projected stung a little, but the deep-seated affection underneath them, coming from man *and* wolf, whether Tala wanted to admit it or not, eased the sting. He'd been honest about his behavior. I couldn't fault him for that.

I hummed and considered ways to help Tala be less grumpy…

"I like being grumpy," he muttered sleepily.

Long seconds later, his breathing evened out, and I continued to take my time rubbing against the soft hairs and bare skin, loving the brush of them over me. Continuing with what felt right, I rolled up one arm, across his chest, and down the other arm. There was a deep rumble and a sigh of pleasure as my skin started to tingle with a funny vibration. With each pass over his body, the vibrations increased and the area where I felt his bite mark sitting just beneath my skin warmed as a strange scent filled the air.

It was all a little disconcerting, not having a clue if I was doing the right thing by continuing when the peel surrounding my innards tightened in the most peculiar way. With it came the urge to roll over his cock, which had remained hard and was dripping onto his belly. If I'd been in human form, I was sure I'd have gulped as I rolled down his stomach, the muscles rippling beneath me even though Tala didn't wake.

The hair at the base of his cock was thicker, and the smell of Christmas spiced nuts increased. I rolled gently over his dick after a little wiggling over his balls to get up onto it. The tightening became almost painful as I rolled up his cock and balanced on the head. The precum coated a little of my skin and eased the tightness a fraction.

Oh, that's how I do it.

Although I wasn't able to grin in my potato form, internally, I was as I figured out what I needed to do to complete the mating. Taking a moment to figure out how best to get the most coverage of cum on me, I rolled off the tip and landed in the pooling precum on his belly. Drips continued to land on me from above, and I groaned in delight as it slid over my skin in the most delicious way. The precum under me soaked me, and I burrowed into the thick hair. Ooh...this was fun.

Wriggling in delight seemed to make Tala's cock happy and gave me a steady stream of precum, so I kept it up.

The low groan from above alerted me that my mate may no longer be asleep, and I was proven right as I was scooped up.

Noooo, I need you to come all over me.

I was eye level with a skeptical-looking Tala a second later, a frown between his dark brows. "Seriously?"

Yes, come all over me.

I sensed his conflicted emotions, but there was also desire. He laid me back just under the head of his cock, and I wriggled to get back into the spot that I'd found earlier. His hand started to stroke his cock, and it was all I could do to remain in my potato form with the urge to lick him.

"You want to taste me, Frenchie?" he rasped in a sexy voice.

I do, but I need you to do this first. I want to have your come covering my skin until it soaks me.

He shuddered, the speed of his hand increasing as he looked down his body directly at me. I wriggled a little as that seemed to please him. The slick sounds of his hand when he reached the top of his dick were drowned out by his constant grunting, groaning, and moaning. Large muscles tensed under me, then he was moving me, and before I could complain, warm cum coated my skin.

I cried out as spurt after spurt hit me and ran over me in a river of joyous delight. The vibrations that had started earlier went into overdrive, and I could hardly keep myself in my potato form. The knowing deep inside that I needed this to bond fully helped me to maintain my form until I was fully coated in cum. Tala ran his fingers over my sticky skin, rubbing the cum in.

Fuck, that was hotter than it should be, Tala rumbled.

It's even hotter for me to be covered in your cum. You smell delicious on me.

He moaned and flopped back on the mattress, his fingers continuing to run over my skin, massaging the cum deep. Before I could think, I was lying on top of him naked and in my human form. The scent of cum was rich in the air, and the cock I was resting on thickened again.

"You're gonna be the death of me," he grumbled in complaint, though it held no heat.

I wriggled, and his cock hardened further as mine rubbed against his. "I've never heard of anyone dying because they came too much. Is that even possible?" I grinned widely at him as he huffed out a disgruntled snort. "Maybe we should try it out. You know, prove the theory wrong?"

He rolled, and I landed on the mattress with a bounce as he caged me in with his powerful arms and a fierce look on his face. My heart fluttered madly as if I had a trapped bird in my chest, trying to escape.

His nose touched the junction between my shoulder and neck where he'd bitten me. The mark tingled with heat and a buzzing vibration that was much the same as when he'd come all over me. He sniffed and moaned. "Smells so good."

Curious, I sniffed the air. "How do I smell to you?"

"Of fries, ketchup, and me."

I giggled. "How can that smell good? Fried potato and come?"

His eyes gleamed with desire as they ran over me, missing nothing. "Don't forget the ketchup," he said in mock horror, showing he did, in fact, have a sense of humor hidden under the grumpy.

My giggles increased but didn't last long as his cock slid up mine as he shifted. "Again?"

His nostrils flared and a wolfish smile appeared. "Again."

Chapter Nine

Tala

My body ached. Every damn inch of me, and if I had the energy to complain about it, I'd—. I rolled my eyes, knowing I wouldn't change a damn thing. Wolves were known for their strength and stamina, but after six days of non-stop sex, I was ready to beg for a break...*maybe*. We hadn't left my cabin because Frenchie decided that he needed to explore every inch of my body in both human and potato form, which had resulted in more sex than I'd had in my whole life.

He was insatiable.

The unique way he'd mated to me had been an eye-opener. He'd insisted several more times that I needed to come all over him in both forms after he'd spent hours rubbing himself all over me. My skin tingled and my cock thickened from the memory. I growled and thumped at it in disgust.

It was weird and kind of kinky.

Secretly, or not so secretly because Frenchie seemed too adept at reading me, I loved it, right along with my wolf. Especially when it changed Frenchie's scent and would warn any other shifter that he was mated. The possessive feelings had increased as the days passed, and with that came this awful feeling in the pit of my stomach at leaving Frenchie alone in the cabin. He'd said he'd be fine, but my wolf was saying differently as it paced continually, urging me to go home. I was starting to agree, especially as the sadness coming through the link with our mate had been worsening as the hours had slowly passed.

The only reason I'd come to work was the call from my brother reminding me of my commitments and that the car I was working on needed to be ready for Christmas. Out of the house, I'd hoped that maybe a little separation would be good to get some perspective. There was only one viewpoint as far as my wolf was concerned, and it was Frenchie should be within our eyesight.

I bit back a sigh, and the sound of the spanner clanging on metal got several wolves glancing in my direction. The uneasy feeling in the auto shop had started the second I'd walked in. A wolf's sense of smell was very acute, and my absence would have caused some gossip. The pack were a bunch of nosy fuckers and liked to meddle in others' business. The nose twitching had been more than obvious as those in the shop had got a load of my scent. Some hadn't hidden their disappointment at the fact my scent indicated I was now mated.

The only two that didn't hide their full curiosity were betas, Redin and Leno. Both wolves spent most of the morning sending me surreptitious glances. They'd both vied for my attention, and though I'd fucked Redin, it had been nothing more on my part than scratching an itch at the time.

I huffed out a loud sigh and pretended not to notice the two beta wolves who'd, over the last half-hour, been slowly making their way toward me. Another twenty minutes passed, and my wolf started to snarl. I growled low and mean when Redin got within four feet of me. "Fuck off, you pair, I'm busy."

"You smell…odd," Redin, who'd always been gutsier, said as he ignored the threat in my voice and came a little closer, his nose twitching.

The uniqueness that was Frenchie would make it impossible for those in the pack to identify what my mate was. My sense of smell was more acute than many, and I'd never have figured what Frenchie was. But then, I'd never have considered that a vegetable could be anything more than a vegetable. Frenchie had dispelled me of that notion.

This morning, my brother had warned me, when I'd met him before the auto shop opened, that my mating would cause concern for some, if not all, of the pack's members. First, because I'd been so damn vocal about not wanting a mate, and second, the weird smell now coming off me. It clearly identified I was mated, but not to what.

Bent over the hood of the car, I eyed the wolf who was treading on dangerous territory right now.

"You got a death wish?" I snared, my wolf getting antsy at the beta being so close to me when Frenchie wasn't nearby.

I placed down the spanner and stood to my full height, towering over Redin. I looked down at him, and he cowered but was stupid and stayed put.

"Redin, I ain't payin' you to stand around all day doin' fuck all. Get back to work," Olowin called out as he strode out of the office. His alpha power notably heated the air.

There was a flash of anger from Redin before he lowered his gaze and exposed his neck. "Sorry, Alpha," he whined. "But—"

He got no further as Olowin leaped over the bonnet of the car in front of him and had Redin by his throat, his feet dangling in the air. He coughed and spluttered as his face turned a dark shade of purple that didn't suit him.

"Did you not hear me?" Olowin's voice got every other wolf in the room dropping their gaze and tilting their heads in submission. He shook the beta hard enough to rattle his teeth before he dropped him to the ground. Redin's boots hit the concrete hard enough to jolt him off his feet. He landed hard and whimpered pathetically.

"Sorry, Alpha," he mumbled.

Olowin's gaze swept the room. "Anyone else feel the need to question my authority?"

There was a chorus of, "No, Alpha," before his dark brows merged and a look of worry replaced the anger when he glanced at me. The concern from earlier returned, and my wolf surfaced.

I faced those scattered around the shop with resignation at having to do some damage control and glared.

"For the nosy bastards who think it's their damn business to know my shit. I found my mate. That's what you can smell. Now you can go back to mindin' your own damn business, got it?" I rolled out a little of my alpha power, hoping to make the point.

Redin opened his mouth, then quickly shut it when Olowin narrowed his eyes at him, his wolf clearly visible in them. "Don't push me unless you want to find yourself as a lone wolf."

Dickwad!

I glanced at Olowin. No one wanted to ever be cast out. It was a fate worse than death for a wolf. We were pack animals, and a wolf's spirit could die from the isolation. *He is, but you've never threatened to kick out a pack member before. What's up?*

The little fucker has been pushing the buttons of some of the other wolves, and they've been complainin'. Let's see if he heeds the warning.

The omega, Cain, who did most of the grunt work, bowed his head respectfully. "Will we get to meet him at the pack meeting tomorrow?"

It was something I'd known was coming, as did my wolf, and neither of us was happy when my brother nodded in answer. "There will be a celebration after the meeting."

It was traditional for the alpha to welcome a mated couple into the pack with a ceremony. This involved the alpha bestowing his blessing on the couple in front of the whole pack after they'd exchanged bites, which were done naked. The blood exchange ritual was one that had stood for centuries. I wasn't sure which part worried me more, the biting or the nakedness.

A sinking feeling developed in the pit of my stomach. Could Frenchie bite and ingest my blood? I didn't want to think about the naked part just yet.

With a building sense of desperation, I opted to speak privately. *This is a mistake, brother!*

One brow arched. Otherwise, there was no other indication I'd spoken to him.

Why?

The blood ritual.

That got more of a reaction. *What about it?*

It's not part of how we've mated. A...

Potato, he filled in helpfully, not hiding his amusement as I growled at him. My wolf surfaced as we faced each other.

His eyes flashed in warning as his own wolf rose to meet the challenge. His alpha power had no effect on me, and I could see his frustration. I yanked hard on my wolf, keeping control, and offered my submission.

The slight tilt of his head showed he accepted my submission. *The pack won't accept Frenchie without it. Figure it out, brother, and be there tomorrow night with your mate.*

There was a finality in his tone, and he didn't wait for a reply. Spinning around, he caused Redin to scramble back to avoid being kicked as Olowin walked around the hood of the car.

There was a collective pause as if everyone sensed there'd been an unheard argument before everyone got back to work. After that, no one looked in my direction as I worked and stewed in my anger. Reason went out the window at the thoughts of exposing Frenchie to the pack and then him being ridiculed, or worse, rejected by those who thought they were superior to other shifters. I chose to ignore that I'd been among them before Frenchie.

How the fuck were we going to complete the stupid ritual? Would Jem be able to help? I reached into my dirty overalls, rubbing grease all over my cell phone case without regard. I searched for the number I'd dialed a week ago. Noise filtered past the need to make the call, reminding me that I was standing in a room full of wolves who all had excellent hearing.

Gritting my teeth, I eyed the half-finished car in front of me. We'd already taken half the payment, and if I didn't want to get my name muddied, I'd need to finish up fast. I shoved the phone back in my pocket and got back to work.

So lost in what I was doing, it took my wolf growling to alert me to the tugging sensation in the center of my chest

Oh fuck.

Frenchie? You okay?

No reply.

Could he hear this far away?

As the feeling of Frenchie's distress grew, I shifted. There were several alarmed expressions as I headed for the door. I heard Olowin swear before shouting after me, "Where the fuck are you going?"

I didn't stop.

Tala, what the fuck?

There's something wrong with Frenchie.

Do you need me to come?

That he'd asked helped settle me a little. *Bring my truck and my phone to the house.*

I closed out my brother and kept my attention focused on the feelings coming through my link with Frenchie. *I'm coming home now. Talk to me.*

The silence was crippling as I was clueless if it was the distance that didn't allow for me to hear him or...

Not able to face that thought, my wolf raced through the town like he'd scented prey. The alarmed face of Donato flashed by when he stepped into my path, and my wolf howled. He jerked back, swearing loudly.

I didn't give a fuck. I had one aim, and that was to get to Frenchie as fast as possible. The animals quieted as I raced through the forest, my wolf on high alert. Within a mile of the cabin, my wolf lifted its head, sniffed then howled in distress. The scent of my mate's blood was strong, and it was fresh. It stopped my wolf from smelling anything else as it invaded his nose.

Fuck! Fuck! Fuck!

There was nothing out of the ordinary outside the cabin. I leaped onto the porch and shifted to open the door. The sight that greeted me left my stomach churning. Frenchie lay naked on the floor, blood pooling around his head. His face was deathly pale, the only color coming from the dark red river running from the wound at the side of his head.

On my knees before I even realized I'd moved, I crouched over Frenchie. My hand shook as I reached out to touch him. Breath hissed through my gritted teeth at the warmth of his skin.

Alive, he's alive!

Chapter Ten

Frenchie

After Tala left, I'd been a little put-out and more than a little anxious at being alone. I wasn't used to it. There'd always been someone around me and alone time was a luxury I was hardly ever afforded. The silence in my head was what was most disconcerting. No brothers nagging at me. That realization had driven me to search for a phone, only there wasn't one in the cabin. Would my family be frantically searching for me? Did it make me bad that I hadn't given them any thought while Tala was all I could focus on when we were together?

The answer was obvious. Slouching, I blew out a big breath.

Would Jem admit to what he'd done?

A shudder ran through me, thinking of the outcome for Jem if the elders figured out what he'd done. They were very unforgiving about certain things. Would this be one of them? I really didn't like the idea of Jem getting roasted and eaten by the elders. Especially now that I was mated and Tala wasn't as put off by what I was.

I eyed the computer on the kitchen table. This one was nothing like the one I'd shared with my brothers. That one was old and wasn't as shiny or as up-to-date as the iMac in front of me. The coolness of the wood under my ass reminded me that I needed to go and retrieve my clothes. The niggling worry about animals doing things with my discarded things was tempered by the reality of what Tala had done to them. They'd be nothing more than rags after he'd ripped them. Still, they were all I had, and Tala hadn't seemed inclined to give me any other clothes. Not that I'd needed any when Tala was here. He seemed to like me naked.

A grin spread over my face at just how entertained he'd been by my nakedness. The wolf, when he lost his grumpy face, was the cutest. Not that I'd let that thought slip out. Years of keeping my opinions to myself made it easy to shield them from Tala. Okay, not all of them. It was hard to keep the naughty ones from slipping through.

The buzz of desire was instant when my head took a detour off in the direction of all the sex I'd had, one which got my cock thickening, thinking party time was back on the agenda. I sighed and eyed it.

"It's not happening. He has to work." My grumpy tone was more suited to Tala than me.

Giggling at how the big wolf was rubbing off on me, I opened the lid of the computer, staring at the multicolored lit keyboard. I bit my lip and shook off the worry that I was doing something I shouldn't be. My sigh of relief when there appeared to be no passwords to get into the email was loud in the silence of the kitchen.

An odd, disconcerting feeling formed at the back of my neck like I was being…*watched*. One glance about the sunny kitchen, and I disregarded the feeling, putting it down to being alone. Going back to what I was doing, I opened up Tala's emails. A grin spread over my face at the last message sent, which was to Jem. I opened the message thread and started to type out a new email.

Jem, this is Frenchie.

Did you let my family know what happened? I don't want them worrying about me. Could you email me back as soon as you get this, please?

Frenchie.

I hit send, then sat in front of the screen, staring at it for the longest time, willing him to reply. In what felt like forever, but was possibly an hour, the computer made a bing-bong noise then a message alert appeared. My hands shook a little as I leaned forward to see who the email was from. I breathed a little easier, seeing it was from Jem and knowing he hadn't been roasted and eaten.

Opening the email, my smile grew wider. *What do you take me for?* I could all but hear him saying it, and I giggled until I read on.

Of course, I spoke with your family. They listen too much to the damn elders, but I stopped them from going to report you missing. They should be happy I found your mate. Folks around here don't appreciate me and my efforts. Damn elders should stop hiding and interfering with what the universe has gifted folks.

I gave Tala a bag of potatoes, though it's mostly dirt for you. I know how accident-prone you are, and I'm not sure if the dirt wherever he's taken you will work in the same way as ours. If you need more, email me, and I'll arrange for Tala to pick it up.

Rereading the email, I stared at the computer. Why couldn't I go get the dirt? Go and see my family to tell them I was happy and maybe show off my mate.

Thank you, Jem. Can I ask why I can't pick up the dirt? Come and see my family?

During the conversation Tala had with Jem on the first morning I was here, I'd paid little attention after Tala had lost his shit at me being his fated mate. What had I missed at the time?

My stomach rolled unpleasantly as I hit send and chewed on my thumbnail, willing another message to pop up. When it did, I wished I hadn't bothered to ask, a wave of nausea coming with it.

The magic won't allow it. The moment you leave the boundary lands, it stops you from returning. I've never figured out the whys or wherefores. It just is. The elders and their damn secrets. They are the only ones who can leave and return. The rest of us are stuck here unless we meet our mate.

Tears dripped onto the keypad of the computer. I sniffed and rubbed the back of one hand over my eyes. I can't go home...*ever?*

I didn't reply. What was there to say? I did want to be mated, but not seeing my family again? That was something I'd never considered. They were loud and were always telling me off, but they loved me. I plonked my elbows on the table and cupped my chin, staring at the screen as a spark of temper grew in my belly, along with the despair.

Jem should have told me about this.

What difference would it have made?

In reality, none. Nothing would have stopped me from going with Tala. However, knowing I couldn't go back, I'd at least have gone and said goodbye. Got one last hug from everyone. My lips formed into a pout, one I'd perfected when I was pissed about something I couldn't change.

So lost in my misery for a second, I didn't notice the odd scent of...*wet dog*. My nose wrinkled at the unpleasant odor that wasn't anything like Tala's wonderful scent.

Getting up, I walked toward the open door. I blinked at the flash of fur, then pain exploded in my head, and the world went into an array of colors. My legs no longer wanted to work, and I crumpled to the floor. Wave after wave of pain made it impossible to focus. My vision blurred, and I attempted to reach out to Tala as the world went white before blackness descended.

Warmth and the scent of Tala penetrated past the layer of fog clouding my head.

What happened?

I could recall him saying goodbye before going to work, but beyond that, the pain in my head wasn't letting me remember more. Why was he cradling me in his lap? He hadn't done that before.

Bare legs shifted under my buttocks, and the throbbing at my temple was no longer all my body was reacting to. The noise I made didn't quite come out as a sigh of pleasure, more a whine.

A worried voice spoke, and the loud words jabbed like a knife into my brain. "What are we going to do?"

My lips wouldn't work to tell whoever it was to keep it down.

"I don't know. I can't get the bleeding to stop. I've fed him some of my blood to see if that will heal him. 'Cause he's so out of it, I can't get him to swallow more than a sip at a time without him choking."

Tala's voice was full of panic, and I struggled to open my eyes, the pain now firmly back in charge. What happened to me? Did I fall? Cut myself? The harder I thought about it, the worse I made the pain, so I gave up trying. What I did know was I needed dirt. It was the only thing that would help.

A memory surfaced. Jem, I'd been emailing with Jem. Had he said he'd given Tala potatoes and dirt?

"Potato...bag...dirt," I mumbled past my sticky lips. It came out sounding more like breathy moans than words. I swallowed, with difficulty, past the coppery taste, figuring that it was Tala's blood.

"Did you hear that?"

"I'm not fucking deaf," Tala snapped angrily, and the thighs my buttocks were sat on, tensed. "Did he say dirt?"

"I thought you weren't deaf! He said potato, bag, and dirt. That doesn't make any sense." I realized the second voice was Tala's brother, Olowin, and that he didn't sound any less panicked or angry than Tala.

"Fuck, it does. In the bed of my truck is a bag of potatoes. Grab it and bring it to me."

There was the sound of boots hitting wood, then a door opening.

"It's gonna be all right, Frenchie," Tala crooned in a voice that was thick with emotion.

My eyelids felt as if someone had laid forty tons of earth on them as I struggled to get them to obey me and open. The need to reassure Tala I'd be fine once I was in the dirt won the battle against the pain. I pried open my eyelids to a mere slit, enough to see my mate and the terror on his tight features.

His gaze held mine and his eyes shimmered. "Frenchie, you listen to me. Don't you dare die on me." He pulled me in tight to his large chest and carefully laid his forehead against the uninjured side of my head. The throbbing made it hard to keep my eyes open, the bright sunlight adding to my misery.

There was more noise and the sound of something thudding on the floor before Olowin spoke. "Here's the sack. What do we do now?"

"How the fuck do I know?" Tala snarled, lifting his head away from mine. I felt the loss and whimpered.

Chills ran through me, and I struggled to focus on shifting. It took longer than normal. The effort left me with no energy to move. I lay still in Tala's lap, and I attempted to reach him through our mind link.

Dirt.

Dirt.

His voice boomed inside my head. *Do I put you in the dirt?*

I cringed. *Yes.*

"Take out the potatoes and leave the dirt in the bag," Tala instructed as he stood with me in his hand.

There was a squealing sound that registered for a second before I was placed into the dirt. Tala's fingers brushed over my skin as he coated me in the magic earth, the magic properties immediately having an effect. With effort, I borrowed a little deeper, feeling the wound inside my skin knitting together. Tala didn't stop rubbing the dirt over me, and I lost track of time.

When Tala's thoughts got clearer, I was able to understand some of them.

I could have lost him. Fuck, I could have lost him.

I sighed in frustration. Some aspects of the healing left me mute for a while, which was frustrating when I wanted to reach out and reassure my mate I was going to be fine.

The longer I was silent, the more my heart ached at Tala's continued panic about whether I'd survive. If I'd been left in any doubt about Tala's feelings toward me, he eradicated them with what he was projecting.

Eventually, I was able to wriggle and move freely through the dirt. Tala stopped stroking me, and I was lifted out of the bag. The second air brushed my skin, I shifted, and Tala caught me in his arms. He peppered my face with kisses, seemingly not bothered I was covered in dirt.

I chuckled at the feel of his stubble rubbing against my cheeks.

He growled and glowered at me. "You fucking scared the crap out of me."

The glimmer of tears spoiled the overall effect, but I didn't take offense, knowing just how upset he'd been.

I snuggled into his hairy chest and sniffed. "I love you too."

Chapter Eleven

Tala

"What...I never said that." I scowled at the top of Frenchie's head, hating that he'd probably felt my heart skipping all over the damn place.

His answer was to snuggle a little closer and run his fingers through the hair on my chest. The tiny, warm hand he placed over my heart felt like he was laying claim to it.

"I didn't," I muttered crossly when my heart kept right on bounding happily along, making me out to be a liar.

The sigh that followed sounded more amused than put-out.

"Shoooo," screeched an unfamiliar voice.

My gaze went to a tiny, naked man cowering in the corner of my living room, who my brother, in his wolf form, was sniffing at. Olowin's whole body shook with what appeared to be excitement.

I blinked twice.

Where the fuck had the guy come from?

I eyed the potatoes lying on the floor with a sense of trepidation growing in the pit of my stomach. *No way!*

So caught up in my fear for Frenchie, he'd been my sole focus, and I'd paid no attention to what was happening around me. Now I could see I'd missed something pretty important. The naked man covered in streaks of dirt could only have come from the bag of potatoes.

"Fucking Jem! He's..." Words failed me.

At my outburst, Frenchie roused himself sufficiently to lift his head off my chest, the sense of loss leaving my wolf edgy. He'd been hard to control after finding Frenchie bleeding. Right now, he blamed me for leaving our mate alone and unprotected. Unprotected from what, I had no clue. Any thoughts that Frenchie had had an accident were dispelled by the threat my wolf sensed.

Frenchie blinked owlishly. "Russ, what on earth? How did you get here?"

The shocked expression Frenchie wore was followed by him bombarding me with loud thoughts, all of which made no sense, with one exception. Brother.

Russ was Frenchie's brother?

Russ didn't answer. He was too busy waving his hands at Olowin as if that would get him to stop what he was doing.

"Olowin, can't you see you're frightening him? Shift for damn sake so he can see you."

Wolf became man just in time to catch Russ, whose eyes rolled into his head as he passed out cold.

Olowin made a choking sound as Frenchie sighed. "Russ has never been good at dealing with anything too complicated. He's nice though. You won't be disappointed with him, I swear," Frenchie said earnestly.

The alarmed expression on Olowin's face was too much, and I started to laugh. "He's your mate, isn't he?" I choked out past the laughter, gaining a growl of disapproval. "Congratulations, brother."

"Fuck you," Olowin grumbled, though he didn't put the little man he was holding down.

Frenchie beamed up at me. "Isn't this so cool? Maybe there are others in your pack that are mated to a potato."

My laughter increased at the very idea of some of the wolves that had definite opinions of mating to anything other than a wolf finding themselves mated to something peculiar.

"I'm not peculiar. I'll have you know that green beans, or maybe broccoli, are peculiar. They can't do more than sit in the dirt or hang from a stalk," he said huffily, then the most adorable pout appeared. He rolled his eyes at me while his lips quivered. "I am adorable."

"Okay, you two, a little help here would be good." Olowin held Russ aloft, staring at the still unconscious man. "Do I need to stick him in the dirt?"

There was something akin to worry in his voice, along with another emotion I couldn't figure out as Olowin was blocking me from his mind.

"No, we only need the dirt if we get injured," Frenchie answered. His hand went to his head. The only signs of what had happened were the blood-matted hair and a thin white line where the cut had been.

My attention back on Frenchie, I questioned him. "How did you cut your head?"

He stilled in my lap, the tension rolling off him obvious without me reading his thoughts. "I'm not sure. I think I was at the computer emailing Jem."

The hand over my heart lifted, and he ran his fingers through my chest hair, looking up at me from under his long eyelashes. "That's okay, isn't it?"

I stared at him blankly. *Is what okay?*

Me using your computer without asking.

"Mates, remember?" I muttered grumpily at the assumption I'd be mad at him for touching anything that was in *our* home.

His head tilted to the side as he looked at me with dewy eyes. HIs fingertips made patterns over my heart. "I've never been mated before."

"You're mine," I growled when my wolf started to snarl at thoughts of anyone other than us being mated to Frenchie.

His giggle was pure delight. "I know that. What I mean is that the elders never said much about what's expected between mates, so how am I to know what's right and what's wrong."

I scratched my forehead. "What's mine is yours and vice versa. It's that simple."

His mouth formed a perfect O as he stared up at me with what appeared to be adoration. I squirmed on the seat, and my cock started to take notice of the naked man in my lap now that the crisis was over.

"Before you get any ideas of leaving me with..."—Olowin shifted his full arms toward us— "him, you can forget it."

"Put him on the sofa then," I countered, watching Olowin closely.

I wasn't disappointed to see the dark look pass over his face as he glowered and did the exact opposite, holding Russ closer to his body.

"Are you sure he doesn't need the dirt? Why isn't he waking up?" Olowin demanded.

Frenchie shrugged. "Russ is a little sensitive. What can I say? It's scary to find out your mate is a massive alpha wolf with a big..."

I placed a hand over his mouth, his eyes twinkling with merriment before they glanced at Olowin.

"Stop lookin' at my brother," I snapped, hating the jealousy swimming hotly through my veins.

"He's right there. Is it my fault my eyes like to wander? I mean, seriously," said Frenchie with another shrug. My wolf was only slightly mollified after Frenchie gave me a kiss. "He's lovely and all, but he's got nothing on you."

My lips twitched, and I worked to maintain the scowl, failing miserably. Frenchie snuggled back into my chest, contentment coming from him. *I can feel how happy you are.*

Oh, shut up.

Giggles bubbled out of him. *Whatever you say.*

It was then that Russ roused and started to strive to get out of Olowin's arms. "What...oh my...you...crap...Frenchie, help save me from the monster."

Being a twin, I was more attuned to Olowin than anyone else. I didn't need our mind connection to know that Russ's rash statement had upset my brother. A blank mask slipped into place, the one he often used to hide what was going on with him. He walked stiffly to the empty sofa and, with care, placed Russ down.

He glanced at Frenchie and me. "If everything is okay, I'll leave you to it?"

I nodded. *We'll talk later.*

The curt nod was his only response as he spun around and walked out the back of my home. Before he disappeared from sight, he shifted, and a howl of distress followed. Knowing my brother, he'd hate that loss of control, especially with the small shifter lying on my sofa all wide-eyed, giving off stay-away vibes.

"You're so silly sometimes, Russ. He's your mate," Frenchie reprimanded with a snap of anger.

"No, I'm going to meet a nice potato," said Russ, continuing to cower. His voice quivered and lacked any real conviction as he continued on. "That's what the elders say will happen."

Frenchie wiggled off my lap, and I let him go reluctantly, though my wolf was back to snarling. *Whatever. He's right there.*

There was an angry growl before he settled, remaining watchful. That was fine. I wasn't going to be letting Frenchie out of my sight again anytime soon.

"The elders are full of shit. They've lied and hidden the fact we have true mates outside of Potatoville." His voice softened as he crouched in front of the sofa, and I attempted to avoid looking at the pert ass that begged to be touched, tasted, and fucked hard.

The scent of arousal coming from my mate alerted me to how loud I was projecting, right before he glanced over his shoulder, aiming a hard stare at me. "Stop it. I can't concentrate when you fill my head with naughty thoughts. I need to talk some sense into my brother."

"No, you don't. I want to go home and forget this happened."

The whiney voice was starting to get on my nerves, and I snapped. "You can't go home."

A flood of tears was his reaction, whereas Frenchie was back to giving me a stink eye. I got up and hated how my stomach was being twisted into huge knots at the displeasure of upsetting my mate.

"We'll figure it out, Russ. But Tala is right. You can read what Jem has written. Once we leave the boundary lands, we can't go back."

I couldn't escape fast enough when the little potato started to cry. With a valiant effort, I kept my thoughts to myself and walked toward the kitchen. The blood smearing the floor brought back the horrors of earlier, not that I'd ever forget the sight of Frenchie pale and bleeding. No, that would be forever embedded in my memory.

Using that anger and fear, I cleaned up the floor and placated my wolf with the knowledge that as soon as Frenchie's brother calmed the fuck down, we would get back to the question of finding out what had happened.

Chapter Twelve

Frenchie

Exhausted after several hours of trying to placate Russ, who was now asleep in the spare room I'd spent my first night in, I went to shower. My stomach snarled from the lack of food. With all the drama between Russ and me, eating had not been top of the list of things to do. The dirt had done wonders to heal me, but I needed food to replenish the energy stores I'd used up during healing.

I sniffed, a tear plopping to the floor, then another. The day caught up with me, and suddenly all I wanted was Tala's big furry body wrapped around me.

As if I'd conjured him, he appeared outside the glass shower door. His dark eyes roamed over my soapy body, and he growled low in his throat. The draft of cool air that came when he opened the door to step inside the steamy shower was never more welcome, with the heat flooding my body. His gaze wandered over my body hungrily, and thoughts of food were forgotten under the want of something else: Tala.

Expecting him to pounce, I braced in anticipation of what was to come, but my eyes widened when all he did was pick up the shampoo.

Pouring a liberal amount into his large palm, he laid the bottle down and held my gaze as he stepped closer.

Water ran over his huge, powerful shoulders and plastered the dark hair to his skin. "I'm gonna take care of you."

My heart quivered in my chest. I sighed in pleasure as his hands started to massage the shampoo into my hair. I closed my eyes and swayed toward him with the gentleness of his touch. The scent of him surrounded me. His large hands washed every inch of me until my legs were wobbling, my cock felt ready to explode, and the slick coming from my ass undid some of what he was trying to achieve. Or I think getting me clean was what he was trying to achieve. It was hard to say with the feelings of being cherished chased by the deep desire for my mate.

He took an eighth of the time to wash himself, then we were out of the shower, and he wrapped me in a large towel, carrying me into the...*kitchen?*

"What are we doing in here? Don't you want...?" A blush rode up my chest, and for some reason, I suddenly felt shy.

He didn't growl at me, though he was scowling in the cutest way when he carefully placed me in a seat at the kitchen table. The place had been scrubbed and cleaned to the point it sparkled in the spotlights placed into the wooden ceiling above us. "You're hungry."

No more was said as he pulled out several large steaks. When they were on the grill, he eyed the potatoes that had come from the bag Jem had given him. "There aren't any more shifters in here, are there?"

Closing my eyes, I opened the senses that allowed me to harvest. "No. They're only potatoes."

When I opened my eyes, I saw the look of relief before I felt it. "Just so you know, you can eat a potato shifter. Some, like me, can regenerate in the dirt if there is still a third of us left."

The hand reaching for the potato hovered in the air, his brows drawing together to form one line. "I could eat you? Seriously?" There was intrigue and, if I wasn't mistaken, horror coming from my big wolf.

I giggled. "I'm told it's the old way my kind mated."

The intrigue disappeared and what came at me in waves was worry. "We are mates?"

The utter seriousness stopped my initial reaction to laugh. I nodded solemnly. "We are. After you bit and fucked me, I realized that it wasn't going to be how I mated to you." I shrugged, unconcerned. "I just went with my instincts because, as I said before, the elders are short on supplying all the information. It worked."

The anxiety went up several notches. "How do you know for sure?"

I frowned and tapped at my lip, projecting what I'd felt when I couldn't put into words the feelings of having Tala come over my potato skin.

A wicked glint appeared in Tala's eyes right before his wolf appeared. The heat of embarrassment was back to flooding my chest and neck but inhaling an arid smell made my nose wrinkle. "The meat is burning."

Tala cursed as he pulled the grill pan out from under the heat. Fat sizzled, and my stomach snarled at the smell, regardless of how charred the meat looked.

"You distracted me," he accused in a miffed voice that caused me to dip my head to hide my amusement.

"Sorry." I tried to aim for contrite, but the snort he gave said I failed. I peered at him from under my eyelashes as he stomped about the kitchen to finish making the meal. His face was set back in the scowl, which I'd noticed was his favorite expression.

I watched him work, staying silent until the meal was plated in front of me. I sniffed at the steam rising off the plate. The steak, a baked potato with cream cheese, and a side of slaw were attacked with gusto.

My plate was nearly empty before Tala went back to the earlier conversation. "How do you know for sure we've mated properly?"

I swallowed the piece of steak I was chewing before answering. "I know how I felt inside. Like I'm connected to you."

The deep lines around his eyes increased. "Then why couldn't you reach out to me when you got hurt?"

It was my turn to frown, and the food I'd eaten started to form into a ball of unease. The memories of what had happened were still a little sketchy, but I had a distinct feeling I'd reached out to Tala before I passed out. "I thought I had. How did you know I'd been hurt then?"

"You were distressed. My wolf and I felt it. It was what brought me home." He shifted on the seat. "If my brother hadn't followed in my truck..."

Tala's look of distress got me off the seat. I tugged the towel around me when he pushed back his chair to make room for me to crawl onto his lap. I met his gaze.

"That has to prove something. If you could sense there was something wrong?" I didn't want to think too hard about if there'd been no soil for me to heal in. "Should we call Jem? He might have more answers for us."

He sighed in what was evidently frustration as one hand ran through his still-damp hair several times. "I think I should...eat you...now. Just to make sure we're fully mated. My wolf is getting snippy with me." He sounded none too pleased at the prospect, yet I sensed a part of him wanted this.

I didn't argue. I got up and dropped the towel, ignoring my arousal that hadn't been my focus while I'd been hungry for food. His gaze dropped, and I worked not to get back onto his naked lap where his own cock was encouraging me to park my ass.

I picked up the damp towel and handed it to Tala. "I think you should cover up."

His grin was all wolf, and I shook my head, squirming when he projected exactly what he wanted. "Behave. If we're doing this, you need to concentrate on something other than sex."

I exhaled shakily, ignoring the slick coating my hole as I dropped the towel over his groin in the hope it would stop tempting me.

He lounged back causally in his seat. "What do I need to do?"

"How do you best like your potato cooked?" I kept my tone serious, but still, Tala chuckled.

"You smell like french fries covered in ketchup to me. That is my favorite."

A shiver of delight ran through me at the deep, sexy timbre and the gaze lingering on my cock. "Okay, eat me like that. You need to grab the bag of dirt before we start 'cause as soon as you've cut off about a quarter of me for peeling, I'll need the dirt to regenerate."

Tala's humor disappeared when he lurched forward, nearly falling off the seat that creaked loudly. "Cut and peel you? For fuck's sake, that's barbaric."

My brows arched up. "How so? You bit my shoulder and drank my blood. Isn't it the same? All you're doing is ingesting a little part of me, the same as you did with my blood. I thought you understood that when I said you had to eat me?"

"Hang on there, I thought I'd take a little bite of you in your potato form. No knives, no peeling, and no damn cooking! Anyway, how is it that I have to do this? Surely you should eat me?"

A bubble of laughter fizzed up, and I slapped a hand over my mouth to stop it from escaping, with Tala glowering at me.

"Sorry," I gasped past the laughter. "I've already eaten a part of you several times and swallowed enough of your cum to float a ship on."

He snorted, not looking in the least bit mollified. "It's still not making sense."

"Do you want to do this or not?" I wasn't bothered one way or the other. It was him who was worried about our mating, not me.

The towel dropped to the floor as he stood and stomped past me toward the bag of soil still sitting in front of the large armchair. He lifted the bag effortlessly and came back.

An unsettled feeling churned the food in my stomach when I couldn't get a read off him, which was a first with how much he liked to project his feelings at me.

The bag was dumped on the chair he'd vacated. "Let's get on with it."

"You don't have to do this," I said, compelled to remind him I wasn't forcing him.

"If this is what has to happen, then we're doin' it now," he ground out, and I barely resisted rolling my eyes at him.

Shifting was easier than getting into a verbal sparring match, so I did that and landed hard on the floor at Tala's feet.

He scooped me up. "You'll hurt yourself, you damn fool," he grumbled.

I'm all right.

His breath ghosted over me as he huffed loudly.

I wriggled on his palm. *A couple of things. First, I can't communicate when I'm healing. Second, I'll sink deep inside myself to avoid focusing on what you're doing. Don't get panicked if you can't sense me.*

"I don't panic."

I didn't bother to point out he sounded panicked now, and earlier too.

Okay. Remember, about a quarter of me should do it.

Chapter Thirteen

TaLa

Why couldn't I have mated to something that could just bite me and be done with it?

Panic levels at an all-time high, I hated myself when the potato on the board in front of me started to wiggle and a sense of hurt bled through our connection.

"Sorry. I'm worried. Can't I be worried about this madness?" I growled with the overriding emotions of alarm at what I was about to do, dancing around inside me. My wolf vied to take control when it sensed my reluctance to chop into Frenchie as I stared at him on the chopping board.

This day had gone from one nightmare to another. Why couldn't I have kept my mouth shut?

Me holding a knife, about to chop and peel my mate, was so not how I expected the day to end! I swallowed hard, my throat working overtime to allow the spit to pass.

"I can do this," I murmured quietly, praying that Frenchie couldn't feel my fingers tremble as I placed them onto one side of him and measured a quarter with the knife. After deciding it was best not to prolong...whatever he'd feel, I shuddered and barely resisted shutting my eyes as I cut a chuck off the potato.

The second the knife hit the cutting board, my heart, along with the air in my lungs, froze. For long seconds I stared at the two bits of potato on the chopping board, half-expecting blood to splatter me and Frenchie to appear howling in distress, missing an arm or something worse. Not that any of those scenarios was good.

When nothing happened, I dropped the knife, recalling how Frenchie had stressed he needed to be put in the dirt. I picked up the bigger bit of the potato and quickly spun to dunk him into the bag of dirt without ceremony. Immediately, I started to rub dirt in the exposed part of his inner flesh. My fingers tingled as they brushed over the exposed part of him, which was softer than I'd expected it to be. I gentled my touch and hoped I was doing the right thing.

When nothing appeared to happen, nerves danced around my belly, twisting everything into painful knots. Fur spouted over my arms. "You were the one in agreement with this shit. I told you it wasn't a damn good idea," I reprimanded my wolf.

"It can take a while for Frenchie to regenerate," a meek voice said behind me, causing me to jerk and drop Frenchie in the bag.

I spun around to see Russ standing behind me, the cover from the bed draped around him, sleepy eyes moving from me to the bag and back. Curls lay in a tangled mess around his pale face and big puffy eyes. "Frenchie is fine."

I eyed him suspiciously. "How do you know? He said he can't communicate when he's healing."

The hint of a small smile appeared, and for the first time, I could see some similarities between him and Frenchie. "I'm his brother. I can sense what he's feeling regardless of how deep he goes to heal. It's a potato thing," he shrugged. "I suppose."

"Oh." I turned back to the bag and found Frenchie had burrowed into the soil. My hands twitched with the need to rummage and find him, but with the weight of Russ's gaze on me, I did nothing.

"Can I have a drink, please?"

I pointed toward the refrigerator. "There's juice in there, or beer. Help yourself."

"Thanks."

There was the sound of feet moving and the swish of material, then bottles rattling while I watched the bag like a hawk. The piece I'd cut off remained sitting on the side untouched.

"Do you want me to cook Frenchie for you?"

The timid question roused me from staring at the unmoving dirt. "Do you know how weird that sounds?"

"Only to you. I'm sure there are things wolves do together that would be weird to us." His tone was petulant.

"Yeah, I suppose. How much longer is it gonna take?"

"I don't know. Frenchie is different from me. We all have unique properties."

I eyed the little man with interest as he sat on the seat next to the bag of dirt. "Frenchie mentioned that. He said he's the only one who can shift with clothes on. Not that he's done that since I...his clothes got ripped."

Russ's puffy eyes widened. "You ripped his clothes?" The alarm came across loud and clear.

My wolf, like me, didn't like the implication I might have done something wrong. "Yes. Why are you looking and sounding like that?"

"Those clothes are a part of him. Where are they? Maybe I could sew them back together." He glanced about as he sipped at the glass of juice he held.

Heat rode up my neck at where exactly the clothes had been left and thoughts of admitting that I hadn't bothered to consider getting them or giving Frenchie any clothes.

"I'll go get them," I muttered. My wolf instantly rejected the idea, but I ignored him. "You watch that bag and don't let anything happen to Frenchie."

His blond-brown brows arched up. "Where did you leave his clothes?"

I didn't answer, pointing at the bag. "Watch over my mate."

Out in the darkness of the night, I shifted, and my wolf reluctantly headed into the forest. He scented the air, and a sense of unease followed. Those pack members who worked in the auto shop often came to the house to drop off things I needed when I chose to work from home in the evenings, which was a regular thing. There was no time to question why the scent of Leno was bothering my wolf as he bounded off in the direction of the waterfall, increasing his speed. All wolf, instincts and senses guided us through the dense trees and darkness.

The coolness of the evening didn't penetrate the thick fur as the joy my animal got from running free took hold. Ears pricking at the sounds of the night, there was a temptation to hunt the prey that thought it was hidden. The night was alive with sounds, and it was a symphony we loved. Hunting was something that allowed the everyday stress to ease, but not today. My wolf was on a mission to return to our mate as quickly as possible.

By the time we reached the waterfall, I was barely winded. The clothes I'd carelessly ripped lay on the ground next to the stone I'd been sitting on. I didn't question why they hadn't been touched by the forest's critters and picked them up in my teeth.

The scent of Frenchie lingered on the material, and my wolf yipped around the cloth before spinning around and heading back through the woods. Exhilarated to have achieved what we'd set out to do, once we got back to the house, I didn't think to shift and came straight inside. At not seeing Frenchie, my wolf whined.

There was a loud squeal, one I recognized.

My wolf, unhappy with the ridiculous noise, snarled at the now cowering man at the counter. Clothes on the floor, I shifted to avoid any more drama. "Stop that crap. You're givin' my wolf a headache and pissin' him off."

Russ sniffed and hugged the cover closer to him. "Sorry...it's all a shock. You have to understand that."

I did, so I kept quiet and picked up the torn clothing, inspecting them.

Shit!

I'd really done a number on them. I held them out to Russ but glancing at the bag of dirt, I hesitated, an idea forming. "If the dirt heals Frenchie, do you think it could fix his clothing since it's a part of him?"

He shrugged. "It could, I suppose. Frenchie has never ripped his clothes before, so it's worth a try."

"Has Frenchie made any moves in there?" I asked as I peered inside the bag, not seeing my little potato.

"No, but he's becoming more alert." Russ nodded toward the potato on the chopping board, which was now peeled. "How do you want me to cook it?"

"Fries, the super skinny kind with lots of ketchup," I answered, doing my best not to think about how weird my life had become. Giving myself something else to focus on, I carefully spread a little of the earth, checking that I wasn't about to suffocate my mate before I buried the clothes in it.

Russ got busy, but I never took my eyes off the bag once the T-shirt and shorts were covered over.

Distracted by the scent filling the kitchen, my mouth started to water. It was so bad I considered going to find something to tie around my neck to catch the dribbles. Once Russ put the plate of fries with a large helping of sauce in front of me, I didn't think twice. I shoved several fries in my mouth, and my eyes drifted closed as I groaned in pleasure.

My senses were overloaded, taste, scent, and texture. They hit me like a bulldozer sending my heart rate into overdrive as I struggled to find my balance. My wolf was all but chasing his tail with excitement as I swallowed the first mouthful.

Was this food porn?

The achingly hard cock, which was dripping onto the floor between my legs, suggested it was. Ripples of desire were continuous as the food made its way through my body. Opening my eyes, I panted past the urge to hump the damn bag of dirt, my hand already reaching for more.

A buzz started at the soles of my feet and worked its way through me until I thought my head was going to pop like a cork from a bottle of the fancy wine Olowin enjoyed. By the time I'd finished eating and licked my fingers clean, the level of desperation to come was epic. The concept of edging was that, a concept, not something I'd ever experienced. Yet, with the sensations flowing through me, it felt like a year since I'd last come. Reaching for my aching cock, I knew one stroke and it would be game over.

"Nooo…you have to wait for Frenchie," Russ reprimanded in a whiney tone that lacked any real force.

I wanted to ignore what he was saying, but the memory of slicing at my mate with a knife—no matter how wonderful he tasted—wasn't something I was prepared to do again anytime soon. Reluctantly, I dropped my hand onto my leg, my balls tightening painfully. I willed Frenchie to hurry the fuck up and heal.

As if he'd read my thoughts, the bag moved a little.

Russ gave me a warm smile and fled from the room.

Chapter Fourteen

Frenchie

Throughout the healing, I'd felt Tala and his mixed emotions on the edge of my consciousness. The conversation going on was more a jumble of static sounds rather than words. Halfway through my healing, I'd smelled my wolf, and it occurred to me as the earth around me vibrated that Tala had gone and retrieved my clothes.

His scent was all over the fabric placed in the dirt above me. After that, the healing, which seemed to drag, sped up. Somewhere at the back of my mind, the thought registered that my clothes were an essential part of me, needed to help with healing. I tucked away the need to share that bit of information with Tala. He'd definitely need to be more careful with them in the future.

Time passed, and with it came awareness, which brought the delicious scent of my aroused mate. I wriggled in the dirt, and as I surfaced, the clothes disappeared from above me. A second later, I was lifted out of the bag, and I shifted, dressed in my clothes.

Tala didn't seem to notice or put me down. His mouth claimed mine in a hungry kiss that stole my breath and made me forget my own name. I wrapped my arms around his neck and clung on. His large hands roamed over me and there was what sounded like a grunt of complaint before he muttered against my lips, "Naked, I need you naked."

When he didn't show any sign of releasing me to let me talk, I aimed my thoughts at him. *Don't rip my clothes, please.*

Those same clothes stopped the large cock rutting against me from touching my skin, making it a temptation to say to hell with being careful.

Need you. Need you now.

I need you to come in my mouth to finish the ritual.

Breathless and more than a little giddy from the lack of oxygen when he released my mouth, I met his stare. Dark desire flared in his eyes. His wolf was there, just beneath the surface. I could feel the energy coming from both man and animal. My heart clambered to escape my chest with the excitement of what was about to happen.

He put me down, and I didn't need any more encouragement. I dropped to my knees, and he growled in the back of his throat as I came forward and licked at the precum coating the tip of his cock. The taste of him flooded my mouth, and I hungrily lapped at the head. It glistened with his precum and my spit as I pulled back and gave Tala a devilish grin. It was the only warning he got as I held his gaze and swallowed him deep.

His eyes hooded and glittered with desire. His features were flushed as his hands came to take hold of my head. I stretched my mouth wide as his cock slid over my tongue. My ass became slick when the head of his cock hit the back of my throat. I choked and spit dripped off my chin, but I didn't pull back. It was overwhelming, the feeling of being owned and belonging to this powerful man and wolf. They were one as his hips thrust forward, and I worked to relax my throat, using my tongue to taste the satiny skin. I inhaled the rich scent of my mate, and I ran my fingertips over the hair around the base of his cock. He juddered, and his hips pulled back. A chuckle was cut off as I followed the move, not letting him escape.

One hand took hold of his hip bone while the other wrapped around the base of his cock to get a better angle. As I sucked him deeper, he grunted and cursed, his hips moving as I slurped and more spit dripped down my chin. The slick sounds were obscene and arousing when he stopped fighting the urges and tried to impale his cock into my tonsils. It thickened and seemed to become impossibly long. I gasped, breathing through my nose as I eased back. My own arousal pulsed painfully, rubbing against the fabric of my shorts.

He growled as I twirled my tongue around the head, giving my throat a break. He cursed and muttered words that weren't any language I'd heard. His fingers dug painfully into my hair, adding to the pleasure coursing through me at his lack of control. I moaned, and whatever that did to my mate's cockhead, he howled loud enough for those in the next town to hear. A second later, warm cum hit my tonsils. Disappointed not to taste him as I swallowed, I eased back. The first few drops of cum to slide over my tongue had my eyelids fluttering closed. The distinct change to his flavor was noticeable.

He tasted of...*me*.

Shivers of a desire so intense they stole my thoughts ran down my spine to lodge in my ass before they merrily skipped to my balls and finally my cock. It throbbed when the extreme urge to bite the cock filling my mouth rose. Instinct took hold, and I bit down, blood and cum filling my mouth as I swallowed, desperate for more. There were more howls, but I couldn't concentrate on those as feelings zinged around my body at the speed of light, leaving me dizzy and floating in a bubble of euphoria I never wanted to burst.

When my teeth finally decided to let go, and I lapped at the still-hard cock, it registered I was aching and hard. The second I released Tala's cock, he was on his knees in front of me, his hands tearing at my T-shirt and shorts. There was no point sighing when I was naked, clothes shredded once more, not when I loved how desperate my mate was for me. Before I could draw breath and demand he fuck me, I was lifted and impaled on his cock. The thickness was perfect as it breached my slick hole, easing a little of the desperation tearing at my control. Desperation that was demanding I throw caution to the wind and insist Tala pound into me before I adjusted to his size.

Both of us groaned as my channel clenched around its prize. The slick made it easy for him to sink deeper and fill me completely. Bright spots flashed behind my eyelids as he gave me a moment more to adjust. One I didn't want or need. I wiggled my ass and squeezed my muscles, encouraging him.

His lips were on mine, his tongue sliding over mine before the sounds of skin slapping skin frantically followed. I lost myself in the driving need to be claimed. Heat started to spread through me, slowly at first, then as if someone had turned up the thermostat on the oven, the temperature inside me increased to the point every cell in my body was burning. The intensity morphed with my body's need to come. I rocked frantically, rubbing my cock against my mate's abs, smearing precum over him.

"Burning, I'm burning," I mumbled through dry lips.

His mouth moved across my frying skin, adding to the heat of the fire. It landed on my mating mark, and I pushed up, hoping his bite would help. As if he understood, his lips parted and he bit down hard. I cried out, ribbons of cum painting his skin and mine. The scent coming from me was different again. My channel clenched tightly, and my wolf moaned, his teeth sinking deeper into my flesh as his cum bathed the inside of my ass for a second time. The effect somehow helped to cool the inferno inside me. I panted and shuddered as he continued to cum deep inside me. My balls worked to give Tala everything they had as the last spurts of cum left my cock throbbing painfully.

I was unsure how long I stayed like that, suspended between pleasure and pain until my ass stopped hugging Tala's cock like a long-lost friend. Eventually, I collapsed forward, sweaty and more than a little exhausted. I rested my head on Tala's shoulder when he'd finished lapping at the bite mark. The skin pinched a little as it closed over, and a feeling of love swamped me.

"I love it too," he murmured into my hair as he nuzzled me in the cutest way, his arm hugging me closer. "Stop with the cuteness thing."

Too exhausted to argue back, or move for that matter, I pressed a kiss to his collarbone, sleep already chasing me into the darkness.

Chapter Fifteen

Tala

After a lengthy conversation this morning when I'd woken to find a very unhappy mate holding his torn clothes, we'd come into town. I'd messaged my brother to say I'd be late for work, not explaining why. There was no way I'd live it down that I was taking my mate shopping for clothes.

Tucked in my pocket after parking, Frenchie kept up a constant stream of chatter.

Can't you keep quiet for a minute?

I immediately felt the now all-too-familiar hurt feeling, instantly pissing off my wolf and getting me in the doghouse. I rolled my eyes. *I'm sorry.*

There was continued silence, and the feelings coming through our link didn't change. "I am," I muttered crossly, feeling put-out. The shifter walking toward me eyed me funnily, then he quickened his pace to pass me.

I scowled and gently ran my fingers over Frenchie. There was a sound of pleasure filling my mind, which was quickly followed by an image of him biting my cock.

Stop that.

Why? You like it. I can feel your body responding.

125

Do you want the wolves around here scenting my arousal?

There was a possessive feeling that had fuck all to do with me, flowing through me, one that got my wolf preening. *You're mine.*

The punch of aggression did nothing to help with my growing problem. I picked up my pace, crossing the street to the one and only clothes shop in the town. Wolves weren't too picky about what they wore.

A bell rang on the door to alert the owner of an arrival as I opened it. In my hurry to get this over with and maybe squeeze in a little naked time before going to work, I forgot who owned the shop.

"Tala, wow. Did hell freeze over?" came the malicious-sounding wolf who emerged from the back of the shop. Lupin, a beta wolf, was immaculately dressed in a pressed button-down and trousers, all in dark brown. His boots, in the same color, shone like a new coin. His blond hair was styled with a product my wolf would have rebelled at. The scent coming from him was cloying and masked his wolf. He cocked his hip and held a pose he probably thought was attractive when in fact, it just made him look lopsided.

The beta wolf acted more like an alpha and spent too much time, in my opinion, catering to his human side. The only time he was in wolf form was when he attended the pack run after the general meeting. Not that I'd paid him much attention, it was all gossip from the auto shop. Some wolves always seemed to enjoy sticking their noses in others' business.

The last time I'd been in here surfaced in my memory, and my mate wriggled around in my pocket.

He hit on you!

Wishing I'd dialed back my thoughts, I masked my features from the wolf in front of me as I worked to placate my mate with the worry he'd decide to shift, naked.

I rejected him.

Lift me out of your pocket this instance so I can look at him.

You don't want to see him.

Why? What is it you don't want me to find out? He is attractive?

I bit back a sigh when Lupin stepped closer at the most inopportune time, with both my wolf and mate getting antsy.

Lupin's shaped brows rose, his lips forming into a sneer he probably thought was sexy. "So, what is it that brought you into my shop?" The sneer disappeared as his nose twitched, and he took another step closer, a look of disbelief replacing it. "Your scent...it's different."

His tone was all accusation, further pissing off my little potato.

This time the sigh was out and quickly followed by a threatening growl when Lupin got within a foot of me, his hand lifted as if he was about to touch. My wolf was ready to snap, and he didn't care if that meant biting Lupin's hand clear off.

Something akin to fear appeared in the beta's eyes before he tilted his head, offering his neck in a show of submission.

Only my wolf wasn't to be placated. "Step back, now," I said around a mouth full of bared teeth.

A moment later, my head was filled with a wave of lust so strong, my cock tried to drill past the buttons on my fly. Lupin's nostrils flared as his gaze lowered, totally getting the wrong impression about what was happening, a predatory light shining in his eyes.

My wolf paced and snarled.

Seeing no way around what was happening, I dug my hand into my pocket and lifted Frenchie out. In the blink of an eye, he stood in front of me, naked, aroused, and spitting mad. He'd never looked more glorious.

He pointed a finger at me, not in the least bit intimidated by me or my wolf. "You can forget it! You are not doing that here, in front of..." He swung to face the stunned-looking Lupin, whose mouth hung open. His wide eyes traveled up and down Frenchie repeatedly, unblinking.

"He's mine." Frenchie pointed to the more than obvious bite mark at the junction of his neck and shoulder. "See. And if you are ever lucky enough to get close to his magnificent cock, you'll see *exactly* where my mate mark is."

There was so much satisfaction in his voice, I found myself struggling to hold my wolf back. It was the appreciative look that appeared when Lupin's gaze once more checked out my mate that got me reaching for the first thing at hand. I plucked up a large plaid shirt from the nearest rail and slipped it over Frenchie's shoulders.

"Put this on," I said, glaring over the top of his head at Lupin. "And you, stop starin' at my mate."

Frenchie shrugged off my touch, and my wolf became insistent that I fix whatever had pissed off our mate. He continued to glower at me as he slipped his arms into the over-large shirt, and I was hard-pressed not to hunch. A level of desperation I'd never admit to fought with the urge to say fuck it and leave the shop now. It was the reality that I'd be in no better position tonight at the pack meeting if Frenchie was naked that had me resisting and glancing at the racks and shelves full of clothing. "Frenchie needs some new clothes. The cost doesn't matter. He can have whatever he wants."

Whatever Lupin had going on in his head, his love of his bank balance won out after a few seconds of hesitation.

"I'm sure I can find something." A calculated look appeared before he walked off to the other side of the shop, allowing my wolf to ease back.

Frenchie sniffed several times and fiddled with the buttons on the front of the shirt, his gaze on the floor between us. "Did you...you know, do it with him?" he whispered.

I didn't tell him it was pointless whispering when Lupin would be able to hear whatever we were saying inside the shop. Instead, I shook my head and tugged him closer. The need to get rid of the sadness that came with the question was my priority. "I'm choosy."

There was a snort of what sounded like disbelief from Lupin. My gaze remained on Frenchie as I pinched his chin lightly to lift it. "At the pack meeting, you're gonna meet some of the wolves I've fucked. It's unavoidable. They were nothing more than something to scratch an itch with."

His lips quivered and his chin trembled. "What about me?"

A deep ache came from how uncertain he sounded. "You're my mate. Mine for all eternity."

He breathed out shakily, his eyes glistening in the light coming from through the shop windows. "Eternity...that's a long time. Are you sure you can cope with that?"

The smile that spread over my face was all wolf and predatory as fuck. "Do you think you can cope?" I projected images of me pounding into him repeatedly.

His cock brushed against my jeans, scenting the air with how much he liked the imagery. A rosy glow filled his cheeks as he squirmed, whispering, "I'm getting wet."

I groaned and wished I'd kept my thoughts to myself with how much I wanted to throw him against the one bit of spare wall and give Lupin a show he'd never forget. Wolves were known for being exhibitionists and didn't really care if they were seen naked or fucking. Having a mate gave me possessive and protective urges, ones I'd have laughed at had anyone even suggested were possible no more than a week ago. Now, there was no way in hell I wanted anyone looking at my mate or seeing how stunning he looked in the throes of passion. That was for me and my wolf only, and he was in full agreement, regardless of how much he wanted me to lay claim in front of Lupin.

When the beta wolf returned with an armful of clothes, I snatched them from him before he could utter a word. "These'll do. We need shoes too."

Lupin made a delighted noise and scurried off once more.

I guided Frenchie to the changing room and handed over a shirt and a pair of jeans. "I'll be right here," I said after taking one look inside the changing room that was barely big enough for me, never mind the two of us.

He was quick to dress, and as the first outfit fit, I didn't suggest he try on the others. Bags and boxes loaded in my arms, we headed back to the truck. There were several interested stares as we headed down the sidewalk. Frenchie spent most of his time looking about, though there wasn't much to see. On both sides of the street, shops were packed with everything anyone could want to buy. The town had grown over the last few years with my brother as alpha. He'd encouraged lone wolves to bring their businesses into the town and join our pack.

My father had been opposed to this, always worrying about having to fight to keep his territory. Olowin was confident in his abilities, and mine, to keep control. I was sure that ability would be tested tonight once the other wolves found out about what I was mated to. I didn't think Lupin had seen what Frenchie was, but that wouldn't stop him from gossiping to the other wolves.

Fuck!

I kept my worry from leaking through our link when Frenchie stopped outside the bakery and gave me a pleading smile. "Can we buy some cakes?"

Chapter Sixteen

Frenchie

I wasn't sure what had come over me earlier in the shop, and I hoped that tonight would be different. Although I wasn't holding out any hope, with Tala's confession to having had sex with some of the wolves I was about to meet.

He'd decided it was best for me to wear one of the new outfits he'd bought me. At least that would protect my own clothes, which had once more been fixed in the soil. We'd still had no time to sit and talk with Russ moping around the house and Tala having to go to work. He'd taken me with him in his pocket, and I'd spent the day with him. I wasn't complaining, not in the slightest, but I could sense his worry while he worked.

Any time I'd needed to go to the restroom, I wiggled, and Tala would go outside to find out what I needed. He was sweet, though it appeared the man had no boundaries as he wanted to stay with me all the time...including when I needed to pee. He didn't get that I'd wanted privacy to use the toilet.

"You're projecting your thoughts real loud." He cast a quick glance in my direction before looking back at the road.

I couldn't get a read off his expression, but that was one of the many benefits of being able to read each other's thoughts. Except when he closed himself off, a habit I didn't like. Not that I could complain. I had used it frequently on my family. However, I didn't like it when Tala was doing it to me.

"You said we needed to talk about what happened at the house yesterday." I chewed my lip when the oncoming car lit up the cab of the truck and showed Tala's deep wrinkled frown.

"I don't think we should do this when I'm driving. My wolf isn't in the best of moods."

I giggled. "When are you?"

The scowl deepened. "I told you I was like this."

The gruffness was tainted with hurt, so I reached out and stroked at his forearm. The hair was soft, and I twisted a little in my seat so I could continue to touch him when a sigh of pleasure filled my head. "I know, and I'm not complaining, just pointing out the obvious. If you don't want to talk about me, should we talk about Russ?"

"If we must."

"Do you think we could ask Olowin to come back to the house and speak to Russ?" A sense of unease followed that suggestion, and I sighed. "You don't like that idea, do you?"

"Nope. I ain't interferin' in others' lives. It ain't my business."

"It is. He's your brother, and Russ is mine. That makes it our business. They are mates, you know it, I know it, and they know it." Seeing I was losing the battle before we'd even started, my mind started to turn over options.

"If they sorted themselves out, we'd be back to being alone in the house." I practiced sending pictures of me laid over the sofa and my big wolf pounding into me.

He grunted and the truck swerved erratically. "Stop that right now," he gritted out through clenched teeth. "You could get us both hurt."

I wasn't quite sure if he was angry or aroused. Both, it appeared to be, when the scent of his arousal became stronger and the hands gripping the steering wheel showed white knuckles.

When he got the truck back under control, he threw me a look I'm sure would have made others cower in fear. I gave him a bright smile. "I'll behave."

"I think hell might freeze over first," he muttered.

He wasn't wrong, but I'd try for him. However, I got distracted when he flicked on the indicator and the truck slowed to take a road that appeared to be no more than a dirt track. The truck bounced along and the trees on either side of us thickened. The air that came through the open window was cooler and there were so many scents assailing me it was hard to separate them out.

"What do you smell when you're with the pack?"

"What?"

He slowed, and suddenly the area opened up.

I didn't look at him. I was too busy having a panic attack at the sight of what seemed to be hundreds of naked men mingling in a huge area outside a massive wooden cabin. It wasn't that I wasn't used to seeing lots of naked men. I was. Just the majority of these men were big and very hairy, something potato shifters weren't. I shivered, and Tala growled as he parked the truck directly in front of the cabin in what seemed to be an allotted space.

"Hey, don't get grumpy with me. It's not my fault there are naked, hairy men everywhere."

The growling worsened, and I shook my head before glancing back to the building, working on ignoring the nakedness for now. The structure was three stories high, and though it was rustic, the way it sat nestled back in the trees gave it a certain appeal. Lights shone through the windows and I could see wood gleaming.

The lower level was a wall of glass and, much like Tala's home, I could see right through the building to the wooded area at the back. The second floor had smaller windows and a large porch with several chairs on it. The upper level was the same as the lower one, with huge glass windows. I had a feeling that the view up there would reach for miles.

I blinked slowly, and my heart started to race when Olowin appeared in the third-floor window. He was dressed all in black. From this distance, I couldn't see his expression, but the way he stood stiffly indicated he wasn't in the best of moods. "Olowin is staring at us."

Tala didn't answer for a second. "He's asking if we brought Russ with us."

I frowned. Why couldn't I hear Olowin? "Do you think 'cause I'm so different from you, that's why I can't hear my new alpha?" For Potato shifters, when the different varieties mated, the lead elders, our equivalent of alphas, were able to communicate with the new potatoes regardless of what type they were.

"I'm not sure what you mean. Olowin was speaking directly to me."

"Mated pairs in Potatoville, when an elder speaks to one, the other hears it." I shrugged. "Isn't that the case for wolves?"

I knew so little, and it was starting to irritate me. The snap in my voice got an eyebrow raised.

"What's wrong?"

"I know so little. It's frustrating. We've done nothing but have sex, not that I'm complaining about that. It's just that we haven't taken the time to get to know each other."

Before I'd stopped, there was a kind of hushed silence outside the truck. *Oops!*

Oops! What the fuck are you playin' at? Everyone can hear you. Fuck, they could probably hear you complainin' in the next county.

There was a sting to his words that hit my heart.

I'm sorry. See, this is the problem. We're newly mated, and I know so little. If you talked to me instead of getting me naked all the time, then I wouldn't keep doing silly stuff that makes you more annoyed with me than you already are. So, until we've talked, there is no more sex for you!

I opened the door and stepped out of the truck, not waiting for him to reply. I glued a smile to my face while blocking Tala from my thoughts. I kept my head up and met the stares aimed in my direction. There was distrust, confusion, inquisitiveness, and several angry expressions. Those, I assumed, came from the wolves my mate had fucked, and I made sure to clock who they were for future reference.

The sound of the other truck door opening broke the silence and eased a little of the tension inside me at being alone in front of so many shifters. I stepped forward, and those closest wrinkled their noses. "Hi, I'm Frenchie, and I'm Tala's mate. It's nice to meet y'all."

Tala was around the hood of the truck and tugging me into his side so fast I staggered for a second before I could right myself. The arm felt possessive. I glanced up, his expression in full *back-off* mode. Undecided if I liked him like this, with my feelings of annoyance remaining, I decided to stay where I was, for the time being, not wanting to cause a further scene.

Olowin appeared from inside the house, and for the first time, I felt the strength of his alpha power pull at me, or that's what I thought it was when I, like every wolf, turned my attention to him. "I expect you all to welcome Frenchie into the pack regardless of the type of shifter he is."

There was some mumbling, and I glanced to the left, noticing Lupin. His lips were moving, and the wolf next to him threw a look in my direction.

"What is he?" Lupin called out, "A bug?" The disdain was clear to hear and got several sniggers.

One minute Tala was next to me, then he was in his wolf form and had Lupin on the ground with his teeth clamped around Lupin's throat.

"Apologize, now," Olowin said in a controlled voice that held a wealth of power. It buzzed against my skin, and I was inclined to say sorry even when it wasn't me he was talking to.

There was a choking sound before Lupin managed to squeak out, "I apologize." His body offered its submission to the angry wolf.

There was a strong sense of unease as attention moved from Olowin to Tala, who didn't seem inclined to let Lupin go.

Olowin's expression didn't change as he walked to where Tala was. "Let him go, Tala. He's apologized."

Lupin grunted in what sounded like pain when Tala obeyed Olowin and released Lupin, taking several steps back. His wolf growled, and the alpha power it appeared I was the only one sensing with every head bowed at Olowin now seemed to emanate from Tala. It was stronger than that of Olowin. I was positive of it. Was Tala a ruling alpha? I'd read that wolves had but one alpha to lead a pack. Was this pack different?

The earlier frustration grew while wolves remained as they were baring their throats in submission and tension crackled through the air, bouncing off my skin. The dirt beneath my booted feet emitted a level of magic that was nothing like home, but I imagined it working its way through my body, and peace followed. Those standing close to me seemed to feel the benefits as they appeared to relax. It was something I'd been able to do since I was a small Fingerling. I didn't understand it, but it was useful, and I'd used it many times to get out of hot water with the elders.

Seconds crept by before Olowin eased back his power. Only then did Tala shift to walk back to me, gloriously naked. He lifted me, and I went willingly, tucking my legs around his hips and holding onto his neck. I snuggled in and inhaled deeply, his clambering pulse slowing.

Olowin came and stood next to us. His voice wasn't loud, but it projected out over the crowd. "Frenchie, he is a unique shifter. One that..." He swallowed and a pained look crossed his face.

When he continued on, I figured he'd been about to reveal more about Russ then changed his mind. In reality, Olowin had been rejected, and I knew how that felt.

Russ, you're a dick, you know that?

My brother didn't respond, but I knew he'd heard me.

When Olowin started to discuss mates, I concentrated on what he was saying, hoping to learn something, anything about my wolf.

A tall, powerful-looking wolf stepped forward and bowed his head before asking Olowin, "What is he? I can't scent him. All I smell is dirt and nothing else."

"Alarick," Olowin acknowledged him, sounding respectful. He glanced around, his eyes narrowed. "Is that not to the advantage of the pack? A shifter with no scent can be an asset."

"That might be so, but what is he?"

There was a look of resignation on Olowin's face before he answered. "He is a potato shifter."

There were gasps and laughter, none of which made my mate happy. I tightened my hold on him. *Think about how you reacted to me. They're no different.*

I never laughed at you.

Maybe not, but sometimes laughter is used to cover disbelief.

He grunted.

Olowin glanced in our direction, one brow quirked up. Tala blocked me from his mind. I felt a barrier lift between us. I got the impression he was having a conversation with Olowin, and I worked on keeping the upset from being excluded to myself.

"Let's see what he looks like," someone called, which was quickly followed by more demands to see me shift.

Tala was back to growling, and Olowin looked none too pleased when he met my stare. The question was there, and as I wasn't worried, I shifted.

The laughter was deafening. I tried to not let it hurt my feelings. I really did. Yet the level of hilarity only seemed to increase when those brave enough stepped closer to a furious Tala to peer at me in the pile of clothes he had held on to.

Then something caught my attention. A smell. It niggled at a memory in the back of my thoughts. I wiggled, and Tala's hand closed possessively over me.

What is it?

I'm not sure. Yesterday, there was an odd smell before whatever happened and I got clocked on the head.

Are you saying one of the pack members hurt you?

The wiggle this time was from the barely suppressed anger coming from my mate, and I debated about how I could avoid answering without lying, something mated shifters couldn't do to their mate. Or it was that way for potatoes. I wasn't sure about wolves.

Can we talk about this after the pack meeting, which we've already delayed?

Tala begrudgingly agreed.

He left me in the bathroom in the packhouse to shift and dress alone. Once happy, I left the room to wander through the house, ignoring those who'd come inside and were staring at me. It was a little disconcerting as no one had bothered to pay me any attention at home unless, of course, I'd caused some mischief.

To distract from the uncomfortable feeling growing inside me, I trailed a hand over the smooth wooden surfaces that gleamed like spun gold. The interior of the house was beautiful and the light played a big part as it reflected off the wood and glass, making the place feel alive. The room encompassed the whole lower level and there were seats everywhere. There was no kitchen in sight. It was as if the lower level's only purpose was for pack meetings.

The forest, much like at Tala's, seemed to come inside the house with the large windows at the back all open. The scents of the forest perfumed the air as I went to take a seat next to Tala, who was watching me like a hawk. The noise in the room increased as it filled.

Tala tensed, and I placed a hand on his naked thigh. The muscles were hard as a rock, so I pressed gently until I felt him relax. My gift was really getting a workout, and I hoped I had enough for the whole evening because I suspected I was going to need it

Olowin came and stood close by us, and the room quietened as he lifted his hand. "It's good to see you all here. Before we get to pack business, I want to remind you all that Frenchie is to be treated as one of the pack. Is that understood?"

I couldn't see everyone, but I sensed animosity. Olowin appeared not to notice when he continued on after several seconds. An uneasy feeling grew and wasn't helped when my mate shut me out yet again.

The niggling memory pushed at me, and I sniffed at the air, my gaze roaming the room. What was it that was bugging me?

$\mathscr{C}$hapter Seventeen

Tala

I'd kept silent about what was about to happen once the meeting was over, and now I was coming to regret it. I wasn't sure Frenchie was going to want to get naked and bite my cock in front of the pack. The relief I'd felt that he was able to bite me and participate in the ritual was short-lived, drowned by the fact that I didn't want anyone seeing my mate naked. That, however, wasn't an option, and although my wolf was ecstatic to show off our mate, I wasn't. It was exceedingly rare for me to be at odds with my wolf, but tonight was one of those occasions.

"Before we head outside to the pack circle to celebrate Tala and Frenchie's mating, if anyone wants to challenge this mating, you need to voice it now."

Fuck, I'd forgotten about this.

Forgotten about what?

The level of trepidation coming from Frenchie was high, and I suspected it was because he'd felt my concern. *Any pack member can challenge you for me.*

What? I'll never win a fight against one of these big brutes!

145

My temples throbbed with how loud he was projecting his fright.

I'm never going to let it happen.

Although Frenchie and I were mated, in pack law, it could be challenged as we hadn't entered the pack circle and bitten each other in front of the pack members.

"I challenge the mating," Leno said.

There were a couple of gasps as I swung around to look for Leno, glaring at the beta who had stepped forward. "You gotta be kidding me," I gritted out through clenched teeth.

The wolf never dropped his gaze, the challenge churning my guts. Leno was one of the stronger betas, and he fought hard.

"I've made no secret of the fact I'm interested in mating with you. You deserve someone strong who can stand at your side."

Frenchie gulped and quivered next to me. *He looks really mad and quite mean.*

The fact he never took offense at what Leno had said showed how frightened he was. My wolf, on the other hand, was furious enough for everyone.

"Anyone else wishing to challenge, speak now?" Olowin sounded resigned.

My wolf demanded I do something to stop this nonsense, but if I wanted my mate to be respected by the pack, then this had to happen. The laws were there for a reason, not that I could see the value in this one right now. The ensuing silence let me breathe a little easier. That was until I registered the level of panic coming from Frenchie, which set my wolf off.

I've never hit anyone before.

Holy fuck. Never?

The sigh he gave was disgruntled, then temper came quickly on its heel. *It's not like we have these stupid traditions. You could have warned me about this earlier!*

"Frenchie, you get to choose which form you fight in."

"I do?" His voice was several octaves higher and hurt my ears.

"Yes, as you have been challenged, you get to decide what form you're in when you fight." Olowin didn't take his gaze from Frenchie.

I'm sensing he's never fought before. He might be better in his potato form so he can evade Leno. Remember, he doesn't need to show dominance. Just get Leno out of the circle to claim victory. Cunning works here.

This is fucked up, and if anything happens to my mate, I know for damn sure my wolf will never mate with Leno's.

Understood. I'll have your back, brother.

I shut him out and, keeping my feelings masked from those around us, I took hold of Frenchie's icy cold hand to meet his terrified gaze.

Choose to do this in your potato form, then you can evade Leno. He's strong and fast, but he tends to tire quickly. You need to get him out of the circle for you to be claimed as the winner.

Albeit slowly, he nodded. *I can do that. Remember, though, I only need a third of my potato to be able to regenerate.*

Less of that! You can do this for us.

His pleasure at the confidence I'd injected into my thought was immediate, and I continued to work on concealing my genuine fear of him getting injured.

The room emptied, and I waited until everyone was outside before allowing Frenchie to shift.

Carrying him out, Leno eyed my hand, and the smug look that followed got Olowin stepping closer to me. *Don't let him bait you.*

Your wolf ever listen to reason when it felt threatened?

Nope.

Then stop talking fucking shit. I'm gonna rip the fucker's head off if he so much as breathes on my mate.

Olowin didn't respond, but I could feel the tension coming from him as he started the challenge by laying down the rules. Once he was done, Frenchie wriggled in my palm when Olowin asked if he was ready. Those closest to us were full of excitement.

The air crackled as Leno shifted into his wolf. He stood over four feet tall, his powerful body quivering as he bared his teeth and growled.

Frenchie immediately started to babble, but the words filling my head made no sense whatsoever. *Wet dog. Ew. He was there. Or maybe all wolves smell like wet dogs. Do they?*

What are you babbling 'bout?

He didn't get a chance to reply as Olowin directed me to put him down in the circle, and Frenchie made a choking sound before he wobbled off my hand and launched himself into the earth. The marking stones that were the circle boundary rocked together, making a noise that silenced the pack.

Leno eyed the circle that seemed to be…singing. The earth moved, and Frenchie disappeared from sight. My heart thudded painfully against my ribs when Leno's wolf howled and leaped into the circle, digging in the spot where there was a mound of freshly dug earth. Before I could move, Olowin placed a restraining hand on my arm.

Trust your mate. Can you feel that?

I could. The earth beneath my feet radiated a power I'd never experienced before.

Yes, but how will that help my mate?

Leno was going crazy. His paws were digging fast and furious. He salivated, the drips falling into the dirt as his mouth foamed.

What felt like an eternity passed before he had a big pile of earth gathering behind him and still no sign of Frenchie. Leno moved and sniffed the earth, and for the first time, I could see the real benefits of having a mate who smelled of nothing but dirt. He'd be impossible to find.

A slow grin spread over my face, and I relaxed, confident that Leno was never going to manage to get his fangs into my mate.

Minutes later, the earth between Leno's back legs shifted and Frenchie popped out of the dirt. My worry for him barely had time to register as Leno walked backward, and Frenchie rolled to the edge of the stones at a speed that made it hard to track him. Leno, in his rush to follow Frenchie, miscalculated, and his two front paws ended up outside the circle.

My grin widened. *You won!*

Frenchie whooped loudly, stopping where he was.

In a flash, Leno snapped his jaw around Frenchie and bit hard. The cry that followed turned my innards to water and my blood to lava. Hot and furious, my wolf emerged.

"Stop," Olowin shouted at Leno. Olowin's alpha power held me where I was. My wolf quivered, and only when Olowin nodded in our direction did we charge at Leno. The one thought was to kill the dishonorable wolf. Leno dropped Frenchie on the ground, succumbing to his alpha. The split-second it took to see the exposed white flesh of his potato was enough to send my wolf into a frenzy. Leno had no time to run before I was on him, using my full weight to pin him to the ground. My teeth sank into the side of his neck, tearing mercilessly at his throat. He immediately offered his submission, but it was too late. Blood filled my mouth as I continued to bite, my paws pinning the big wolf, not letting him escape the inevitable.

Olowin's voice barely penetrated past my fury. "He's dead. Stop, Tala, you've made your point. Your mate needs you."

The latter part got my wolf to see reason, and he released the dead wolf. I didn't acknowledge Leno, who was covered in blood, his fur and flesh torn from his body. I tipped my head back and howled a warning. The alpha power I'd never wanted surged within me and burst forth.

Every wolf, except Olowin, offered their submission.

I snarled and snapped at those too close to the circle as I went to where I'd last seen Frenchie. The threat to my mate made it impossible to get my wolf to recede. I sniffed at the ground and easily found where Frenchie was. Gently, my wolf dug him out, nose rubbing all over his skin, assessing the damage. There were still puncture wounds that incensed my wolf, who cast another eye at Leno.

Home, we need to get home.

Jaw opening wide to collect Frenchie, my wolf was off and running for the trees in the direction of home. Those in the way jumped aside to avoid being trampled.

Olowin was there beside me seconds later. *What do you need?*

There is dirt at the house. It will heal him.

Twigs and branches caught in my bloody fur as my wolf took the quickest route home. In half the time it would have taken if we'd come in the truck, I was home. My wolf leaped straight into the house and charged past an alarmed-looking Russ, who appeared from the hallway.

Olowin's groan sounded pained as he followed. The worry about what was going on with him and Russ wasn't something my wolf cared about. The bag of dirt we'd left sitting on the floor next to the closet was all my wolf was concerned about.

The scent of dirt increased as my wolf stuck his head in the bag and gently laid Frenchie down. The second he burrowed in, I shifted. More aware of the coppery taste of blood in my mouth and the flakes that had dried on my skin, it was harder to ignore what had occurred. My hands shook as I reached in, needing to touch Frenchie to reassure me and my wolf he was okay.

Frenchie, are you all right? Frenchie, answer me?

I rolled my eyes heavenward at my own stupidness, recalling what he'd said about when he healed.

"How's he doing?"

I glanced at Olowin from my crouched position. "He's healing, I think. When he's doin' that, he can't communicate with me."

A deep frown appeared between Olowin's dark brows as he looked at the door and at Russ, who was hovering. He wasn't panicking this time, which was a small blessing, but I wasn't sure if that was because he had something else to look at. Namely, a naked Olowin, his cock hard and leaking. There was no way to hide how his body was reacting to being in close proximity with Russ.

The dirt I was touching moved, and I switched my attention to the bag in front of me. "Frenchie, you okay?"

No reply.

I grunted in frustration.

I wasn't sure how much time passed before there was more movement, but I released my first easy, shuddering breath. My knees dropped to the floor, and there was the sound of feet padding over wood, then a door shutting. I never took my eyes off the inside of the bag and the mound of moving dirt.

"Come on, Frenchie, heal goddammit!"

There's no need to shout. I'm not deaf.

My relief was immense. I couldn't respond. I scooped him out of the bag, and a second later, he was sitting in my lap, dirty and looking amazing. I brought him to me and kissed him with all the wealth of emotions surging through me.

He pulled back, his nose wrinkling. "You need to brush your teeth...you taste of...Leno."

He shuddered, and I couldn't help the laughter that came at the horrified look when his gaze dropped to my filthy chest. I could only imagine how I looked to him.

"No, make that a shower." He wriggled off my lap, which got my cock taking notice. "And you can forget the sex part. I haven't forgotten you're in my bad books." He stomped toward the bathroom, his little ass flexing.

I got up off the floor, my wolf demanding we go fix this. I blew out a breath and walked after Frenchie, hunching at what I was about to do: apologize.

There was nothing worse!

Chapter Eighteen

Frenchie

It had been four days since the incident at the packhouse, and we were yet again on our way there to finish the ritual, which Tala had explained once he'd apologized. After that, the no-sex rule lasted the length of the shower and long enough for Tala to brush his teeth.

He'd needed to reassure himself I was fine no less than seven times that night, not that I was complaining. It had given me something else to think about other than the realization I'd had about Leno. Tala had questioned me when he'd taken a breather in between bouts of sex and eating, both of which I couldn't seem to get enough of. When he'd asked what I'd meant about *wet dog* when Leno had shifted, the memory of his scent had returned. It had been hard to keep my reaction to myself at Tala's explanation that all wolves had their own unique scent. No two were the same.

I was positive I'd smelled Leno in the house before I'd lost consciousness after...well, I still hadn't figured out what, but somehow Leno was involved. Maybe? And that was the issue, I couldn't say for sure, which made for a hard conversation accusing a dead wolf. Would telling Tala that make a difference? The wolf was dead because he'd cheated.

Was holding back like lying by omission?

It was a difficult one, so I'd decided to leave talking about it until after the mating ritual tonight.

Focusing back on the events of the evening, I asked what had been on my mind since Olowin had called to say he'd arranged for the ceremony tonight. "Can anyone else challenge me?"

I worried my lip with my teeth, the puffiness alerting me to how long I'd been chewing on it already. My thoughts drifted to what was planned as I eyed the bag of dirt at my feet. Tala was taking no chances with me. It was sweet but also a little terrifying, with fresh memories of Leno's teeth sinking into my flesh. The shock and pain had immobilized me.

Russ coughed loudly, allowing me to shove what happened to the back of my mind. I looked over my shoulder. He had on one of the outfits that Tala had bought me because we were the same size. If I wasn't mistaken, he'd taken extra care with his hair. He'd insisted on coming tonight too.

How Olowin was going to react to Russ's presence was anyone's guess. "What's botherin' you? You were the one who insisted on coming."

I wasn't sure myself what to make of it when Russ blushed and averted his gaze to the window. He'd come and sat with me to listen to Tala talk about wolf culture and the laws of the pack the day before. Tala was getting better at talking, which he grumbled about more often than not, though that didn't stop him from sharing. There was so much to being a wolf, with lots of rituals and laws associated with the pack. Some of which, like the one we were about to participate in, was...weird. The idea of biting Tala was fun. Doing it in front of the pack, not so much. Potatoes weren't exhibitionists, and things that happened between them that were connected to sex were done behind closed doors.

Tala answered my question when Russ remained silent. "No, they had their opportunity. It'll all be fine."

"Yeah, like I'm used to biting a cock in front of a pack of wolves."

He growled, and a shiver of desire at his possessiveness did crazy things to my ass and my stomach, which seemed to have spent the last two days undecided about everything. I rubbed at my belly, which was a little bloated and tender.

Tala glanced at me and down at my hand before switching his attention back to the road. "What's up?"

"My stomach. I feel queasy, but then why wouldn't I?"

He sighed, his dark scowl back where it lived when he was doing his best to appear unconcerned about me when it was the exact opposite. I'd been paying attention to my mate, which was easy when he never left me alone, not even when he left to go to work. I was no longer assigned to his pocket, and

I'd been allowed to roam freely around the auto shop. He'd even taken the time to explain some of the things he was doing.

A warmth spread through my chest and settled in the pit of my stomach, easing some of the unsettled feelings.

"After tonight, it's done. Then things can go back to normal."

I rolled my eyes at how he stupidly thought I'd want normal. He was the best thing that had happened to me. "Nothing has been normal since you appeared in my life."

I swallowed hard, struggling to say more when a wave of nausea hit me so suddenly I shot forward. The seat belt pulled tight over my chest and lower belly, and vomit surged up into the back of my throat. It burned as it spewed out my mouth and nose in the footwell of the truck. The stench made it worse in the heat of the cab, causing another wave of nausea to hit me. Sweat beaded over my forehead as my stomach heaved and more vomit splashed at my legs and booted feet.

"For fuck's sake!" The truck shuddered to a screeching halt. Out of the truck in a flash, Tala charged around the front before the next wave could release its vengeance on the truck.

More gently than I'd expected, he released my seatbelt. That, I thought, was a dangerous game he was playing with how uncontrollable my stomach was. The next two bouts came fast and furious, the same as the last two. One arm was around my middle while he rubbed at my back as I bent forward and decorated the side of the dirt road.

The shirt I wore was soaked with sweat, and I was only standing because Tala was holding me up. Weak but feeling decidedly better, I let Tala hold all my weight. "That was unexpected. I don't think I've ever been that sick before."

The moment I spoke, I realized I'd made a mistake as a flare of panic hit me full force from Tala. Lifted bodily, I found myself back in the truck, staring at the pale-looking Tala. I was strapped back in next to Russ before I could get my mouth to work.

"What is the matter? I was the one who got sick."

Russ nudged me gently. "You dork! That's what his problem is." He shook his head as Tala returned to the front seat, and we took off so fast I was shoved back into the leather of the seat.

I swallowed, praying my stomach would behave. "Tala, slow down. I might get sick again."

"We need to get to the packhouse and see the doc." He did the exact opposite, and though I was thrilled he was so concerned for me, my stomach wasn't sure it could take much more.

I shut my eyes and stopped looking at the road as it flew by. I breathed deep, then regretted it when all I could smell was my own vomit coming from my clothes and the front of the cab. Water gathered in my mouth, and I did my best to swallow it back and not think too hard about the nasty taste in my mouth. By the time we got to the packhouse, I wasn't sure how I was feeling. A part of me was hungry, which was simply wrong after I'd puked.

Russ chuckled.

I pried open my eyes to see what was amusing him. Tala, who looked more than a little wild, stood outside the truck, arms flapping and lips moving, though there weren't any words coming out.

Reaching out to see what his problem was, I was met by a wall blocking me from his thoughts. There were two options. First, he was conversing with Olowin, which was likely. Or second, he'd gone into complete panic mode, which was something else I'd noticed about him. When he didn't want me to know he was distressed, he shut me out.

A figure lumbered out of the cabin. He was huge and had a wealth of gray hair covering his head and his lower face. The beard hit his chest. His eyes were…kind. He came past Tala and opened the truck door, his gaze assessing as it swept over me.

"Frenchie, I'm Doc. Can you tell me what's ailin' ya?"

I breathed out and gathered my thoughts. "I'm not sure. One minute I was fine, next I was pukin' as if aiming for a world record."

He chuckled. "Let's get you into the house so I can check you out." He'd no more than reached to unclip my seatbelt, and Tala was snarling.

"I'll do it," I said to Doc while I glared at Tala. *Stop that, he's only helpin', and* you *were the one that asked him to help.*

There was a disgruntled snort, but he backed up and let Doc help me into the house. He led me past a pack of wolves that nodded but kept their distance. Up the stairs to the second floor, which Tala had informed me was Olowin's home, he helped me to a plush-looking mustard sofa.

Out of the truck and sitting, I was starting to feel a little like a fraud when my stomach started to snarl, wanting food.

"You feeling hungry?" Doc asked as he settled me on the sofa.

A wave of heat rode up my neck, and I avoided looking at Tala, who was leaning against a wall watching Doc. "Yeah. I mean, how can that be?"

"Let's have a little look at you."

He got me to lie back and asked me several questions, none of which made any sense. "I don't know what you mean by a heat? I feel hot and sweaty, but that's from the vomitin'. I think."

His brows arched when he glanced over his shoulder at Tala. "Don't...potatoes have a heat?"

"How the hell would I know?" he snapped angrily, but there was also a world of worry coming from him.

"What's a heat?"

Doc scratched at his beard and took the seat next to me. "Can you tell me how your kind produce young?"

Ignoring the panic that Tala didn't seem to have any control of, I tried to concentrate on Doc. "Potatoes have...sex," I squirmed a little, feeling all sorts of embarrassed at talking about this stuff. It was like having an exam, and I was crap at those. "If it's the season for planting a new crop, that is the time that a potato can make a family."

Doc's thoughtful expression became intrigued. "How often is that?"

"Once a year for a month. Planting season, really."

"When was the planting season?"

"It's in a couple of months' time. Normally the beginning of spring. Why?" Again Doc didn't answer me but gave Tala a look I couldn't interpret. "I'm right here, you know. Will someone explain what vomiting has got to do with seasons, heats, and..."

Two and two became four and my mouth dried at what number popped into my head. I cupped my belly, looking at both wolves. "You...think...I'm pregnant?"

Tala jerked as if I'd kicked him in the nut sack, and Doc grinned. "Yep, I think you might be pregnant. But to make sure, I'll need you to come by my place, and I'll do a scan."

"A scan," I rasped and swallowed. Dizziness hit me forcefully, and I shut my eyes, lying back on the sofa. I was pregnant! I was going to have...oh jeez!

"Pregnant, no fuckin' way. I'm not ready for this!" Tala stomped back and forth in front of me.

"We've only been mated for two damn seconds. How the hell can you be pregnant? Is this some sort of potato magic that you never told me about?" he snarled.

"Well, that told me!" I didn't attempt to hide how hurt I was.

Chapter Nineteen

Tala

"You'll do anything to avoid the ritual," Olowin said from his position, sitting behind his large office desk. "However, this is even a bit dramatic for you."

The third floor of the packhouse was split in two. Olowin had converted the back part into his office for pack business, and the front half was his bedroom. It had an amazing view of the mountains off to the west. Our fathers had a house in town, and that was where Dad had remained after Father died. He preferred the company and busyness of town. He was a bit of a social butterfly. Olowin was much like him, whereas I was more like Father and preferred to have my own space away from folks.

When the packhouse had been built, I believe Father chose this spot for that very reason, to get some distance from the town. He'd been thwarted by Dad, who wouldn't budge on moving.

Was I going to be like that with Frenchie, always giving in? My wolf couldn't see a damn thing wrong with that, and if I was honest, I was coming to the realization I couldn't either.

"Why are you giving me the silent treatment? It's not me who has an annoyed mate."

"No, you have a mate who isn't interested in you," I snapped back. I regretted it immediately, seeing the pain he didn't hide from me. "Shit, that was low even for me. I'm sorry. This whole pregnancy thing has thrown me."

I plonked myself down in the seat opposite my brother and buried my head in my hands.

"It's fine. I know you weren't being intentionally cruel." His voice was clipped. "It isn't confirmed yet. It might just be that he ate something that didn't agree with him."

It was all my wolf's fault. The minute Doc had started to question Frenchie, my wolf had surged forward and one sniff had confirmed our mate was pregnant. Why couldn't I keep my big mouth shut? I'd hurt my mate. Olowin was right about that.

I shook my head as I looked up and dropped my hands. "Nope, my wolf says he's pregnant."

The terror that I'd felt earlier, that got me opening my big mouth and talking shit, had receded a little, and I was...*excited*?

"You don't sound very happy?"

I arched my brows. "I've barely had time to adjust to all the damn feelings I've got churning inside me. Now there's a whole load more, and I'm fucking drowning in them."

I got up and started to pace, making sure to check I wasn't projecting my thoughts to Frenchie, who was downstairs with Russ and Doc. He'd remained on the second floor, which I was banned from after making him cry. Russ might be a little wimpy, but he was a fierce protector of his brother and hadn't been in the least bit shy in shoving me out of the room.

The only reason I'd gone was that Frenchie seemed to think he needed space from me. That had come across loud and clear, not that I blamed him. My outburst had hurt him deeply. I couldn't ignore it, even if I'd wanted to, which I didn't. Easier to leave them be for the time being. I'd gone to find Olowin to explain tonight was not happening.

The pack had been their usual, interested in details I wasn't about to share. And if I was honest, I was hiding out, unsure I'd be able to control my wolf if anyone made so much as a snide comment about my mate if they figured out what the problem was.

"It must be hard, Tala, but imagine what it's like for Frenchie. If what you say is correct, then he's pregnant with no clue how his body is going to behave. You need to reach out to the dude who sold you the transmission and see if he can help."

I stopped in front of the desk and eyed Olowin. "I think I need to go there. The guy is cagey, and I think I'm gonna need more dirt. I've no clue how long the stuff I've got will keep healing Frenchie, and after everything that's happened, I ain't taking any risks."

For the first time this evening, Olowin grinned. "Love suits you, brother."

"Fuck off." It was the best I could come up with when my wolf preened and my heart danced around my chest in fucking agreement.

The following morning my mood was worse, and everyone was avoiding making eye contact with me in the small waiting room I was pacing around. We'd arrived twenty minutes earlier at Doc's, and I'd been banned from going in with Frenchie. He'd been kind enough to tell me to *fuck off* through our link rather than humiliate me in front of other pack members, who watched with interest as he disappeared into Doc's examination room with Russ.

"Something wrong with your mate?" Tundra, an old alpha wolf, asked when the door shut in my face.

The hard stare I gave the room got the three other wolves shrinking in their seats. Tundra didn't so much as move a muscle. The wolf had balls. I'd give him that. "None of your damn business."

Tundra shrugged, looking unconcerned as he picked back up the magazine he'd been reading. "Suit yourself."

There was a snigger from a young wolf who was sitting on Nomad's lap. The boy had to be about seven or eight and had two missing front teeth. He was...cute.

What would our babies look like?

Pretty babies with curls and Frenchie's blue eyes? My wolf loved that idea.

An emotion washed through me so strong, it nearly bowled me over. Before I could register what I was doing, I barged into the room Frenchie was in. All the occupants stared at me, but my eyes were drawn to the tiny monitor where there were a couple of blobs on the screen.

Russ came past, giving me a hard stare before the door clicked shut behind me. I didn't move. I couldn't when the blobs on the screen moved once more.

Frenchie let out a small sob, and that released my feet. Across the room, I reached for his hand and clasped it tightly. "Look...pups."

Doc was grinning. That had to be good. "Looks like. You've got two in there."

Frenchie shuddered, and the hand holding mine clenched tightly. His eyes shimmered. "How...what...oh god...what am I going to do?"

There was excitement and terror in equal measure coming from him. The reality of seeing my babies was nothing like I'd expected it to be. Last night it had just been a concept that had no substance. The screen and the moving blobs changed all that.

Fuck, I never thought I'd have a family.

A gut-wrenching sob from Frenchie brought panic. "What is it? Are you hurting? Do you need a doc?"

Chuckles came from behind me, and I couldn't understand what was funny with Frenchie so upset.

"Do you want a family?" Frenchie hiccupped past the next sob. Tears rolled down his pale cheeks as his eyes begged me.

Fucking hell!

"Shit, you read me wrong. I didn't mean I didn't *want* a family, just that I'd never considered I'd have one. I didn't think I'd end up with a mate. Now we're gonna have babies."

More tears came, and it appeared I was making things worse. My wolf was pacing and snarling at me. Doc's grin got bigger as he ran the thing he held over Frenchie's belly, making the blobs change shape.

"I didn't expect any of this either." He sniffed. "It's not your body that has to...oh god, how do you get them out of me?"

He looked at Doc, and if it was possible, his already pale cheeks went a shade of white that made him appear deathly ill.

My throat closed over as Frenchie started to fill my head with horrific images of what he thought was going to happen. I glared at Doc.

"How?" I swallowed so hard my throat clicked.

"I'll need to do a bit of research on that." He wiped the gunk off Frenchie's belly and pulled down his top. "Is there a doc in your town?"

There was more sniffing from Frenchie, and Russ stepped to the couch. "There are a couple.

You'll want Doc Picker. He deals with the...birthin' of Fingerlings."

My knees turned to jelly. "Will there be a problem with the two species mergin'?"

It was the only way I could think to put it, and that appeared to set off my mate again.

"Oh god, what if...?" A howl of distress was cut off as he twisted and buried his head in my stomach, his hand releasing mine to move around my waist and hang on.

"We'll figure it out. I've never lost a pup, and I don't intend to start now." Doc's voice was full of confidence.

Once we had another appointment booked for the following week to check the progress of the babies and a prescription for vitamins, we left with me carrying a tearful Frenchie to the truck. At home, he vacillated between laughing and crying, appearing not to know what he was feeling. When Frenchie had gone to pee and Russ had gone to fill the prescription, Doc had explained that Frenchie would get emotional. Hormonal shifts in the body were to be expected, but he'd said it would happen in the next few weeks, not right away.

Anxiety held my rational brain hostage as I listened to Doc tell me for the seventh time that day that everything was fine and that if I called him again, he'd block my number. I slammed my phone down on the counter and cursed.

"Shush, Frenchie has just gone to sleep," Russ said in a harsh whisper.

I glanced at the sofa where I'd placed Frenchie when we'd gotten home. He was wrapped in a large snuggle blanket I'd bought before leaving town. One similar to the one my dad used when he wanted to feel comforted. His eyes were puffy from all the crying, but he looked peaceful. I nodded at Russ and went to sit at the kitchen table where I'd placed my computer. "I'm gonna email Jem to see if he can get some information for us."

Russ sat on the seat next to me, sucking on his thumb as he stared at the computer.

We sat in silence as I thought about how to phrase what I wanted to ask.

"Can you ask him if he knows of any way I can go home?"

"See, this is why I don't do folks. They always want you to get involved in their business." I reacted as I usually do, without thinking, and now I was paying the price as Russ started to sniff. I pointed at him. "Don't you do that! I've had enough tears to last me a lifetime."

He sniffed again but appeared to gather himself.

I groaned. "Listen, my brother will be a good mate."

"He doesn't want me," Russ whined.

Give me fucking strength! "You rejected him, hurt his feelings. What did you expect him to do, fawn all over you? Forget it. Wolves have long memories, and you not only rejected Olowin, you also rejected his wolf."

His chin trembled, but I gave him a ten for effort when he didn't cry. "Do you think there is any way I could make it up to him?" His hands fluttered on the table in front of him.

The sinking feeling at the knowledge I was screwed grew. "You'll need to show Olowin you can be trusted not to hurt him," I gritted out.

His lips parted, and I shook my head. "I ain't sayin' no more. You figure it out."

In desperation, I grabbed at the lid of the laptop and opened it, hoping he'd get the hint and stop sharing his problems with me.

Chapter Twenty

Frenchie

Nausea came and took up residence, and it didn't seem to understand that I needed a break from staring at the bottom of the toilet bowl. I wiped at my mouth for the tenth time and sat back, considering if it would be easier on my knees to get a bucket and place it next to the sofa.

There was a noise behind me, but I didn't bother to turn when I smelled Russ. Tala had gone to Potatoville to get more dirt and meet with Doc Picker. He'd taken Doc with him so he could ask more questions about my...pregnancy.

A shiver ran through me, and Russ draped a soft fleece blanket over me. "Do you need me to help you up?"

I nodded, too tired to speak.

Russ placed an arm around my back and led me to the sink so I could brush my teeth. I didn't look at the hollow-eyed person in the mirror as I used the towel to dry my lips. It had been a full week since I'd been told I was pregnant, and my body had done nothing that the textbooks or internet said should be happening. The sickness right now was the worst thing to deal with. It hadn't given me a moment's peace. Morning

175

sickness, they called it. They lied! Mine was morning, noon, afternoon, and night sickness, all damn day every day. My body ached from how much time I'd spent bent over the toilet.

That didn't seem to stop my belly from swelling. I felt like I was the size of a house. All the pregnant Fingerlings I'd seen had only had tiny swollen bellies, nothing more than that. I glanced down at mine and huffed in frustration.

"It's going to be fine. Tala will get answers today."

The fear I worked hard to keep at bay, thinking it couldn't be good for the babies, crept past my defenses. "What if he doesn't? What if something happens to my babies? What if—"

"Stop. You know what Tala said about traveling down the *what-if* road. That will only lead to upset. And I, for one, would like to keep my ass from getting kicked if he starts to sense you're upset and can't get back to you."

The words had barely gotten past his lips when a phone started to ring in the other room. I rolled my eyes heavenward and prayed for patience. It was a fifty-fifty chance with how topsy turvy my emotions were. "Go answer it. He'll only stress if you don't."

I'm fine, Tala.

Answer the damn phone. I want to hear your voice.

I trudged after Russ, the blanket swishing around my bare legs as I headed to the sofa, trying

176

to figure out what I was going to eat. The hunger always came after the purging. I held out my hand when Russ brought the phone to me, mouthing the word sorry as he put it in my palm.

"I'm fine. Don't start, please. I don't have the strength to argue."

There was a loud growl. "I knew it was a mistake to leave you."

"I mean it. Stop, or I'm gonna put the phone down and block you from my thoughts." The threat was real, and I sensed him weighing the possibility I'd do it.

"I'm worried."

I sank into the seat and tugged the blanket closer, missing the feel of his arms around me as I wallowed in my misery. "I know. But if you stopped frettin', you'd get to Potatoville quicker and then be able to return and see for yourself I'm fine."

The snort said he didn't believe me. Doc had been emphatic about me not shifting without knowing the effect on the babies. Without the option of the normal way of finding peace and making myself feel better, I wasn't able to help my body.

"Please, I need you to figure out what is happening, so we know what to expect. I'm fine here with Russ, and you have Olowin checkin' in with us every five minutes." I sniffed. "I love you."

I love you too.

I chuckled at how he sent it as a thought. "You're funny. Go on now. I'll see you later

177

tonight." I didn't give him a chance to answer. I flicked at the screen, then switched the phone off and closed him out of my mind. I needed a break.

Russ's brows rose.

"He'll call again. He won't be able to stop himself, and I'm exhausted from the pukin'." I lay down and tucked the blanket under my chin.

"What do you want to eat this time?"

Over the last few days, the combinations I'd subjected my body to through my bizarre cravings didn't bear thinking about. "Potato soup with a big dollop of chocolate ice cream in it."

The shade of green Russ went got another exhausted chuckle. "I'm never getting pregnant," he muttered, disappearing off to the kitchen.

My eyelids drooped and I closed them. I'd rest for just a few minutes.

It was pitch black when I opened my eyes, feeling a little disoriented when I tried to adjust to the lack of light. What time was it? Had I slept all day? The soft mattress under me suggested I'd moved, at some point, from the sofa to the bed, but I couldn't remember doing it.

About to sit up and check the time, I inhaled and stopped at the scent of my mate. A smile formed on my lips when a protective hand moved over my naked belly. I twisted my head on the pillow, barely making out the figure lying next to me.

Although he tugged me closer to him, his breathing was deep and even. Warm and protected. Those were the two prominent feelings that came from him. They were quickly followed by a deep sense of love. One I suspected he'd never truly admit to when he was awake. He was a grump, there was no denying it, yet there was a well of love inside him. Though it might not always be expressed in a positive way, it was there nevertheless.

His actions were how he conveyed his love, and I was coming to understand it and accept that. I didn't need him to say the words. The two blobs inside me twirled around as if they were trying to dance together, demonstrating their full agreement.

I bit my lip to stop the giggle escaping at the silly notion they could read my thoughts. Light snores broke the silence, and I lay in the dark, letting them lull me for a while. After a time, the blobs decided to act up, and I slipped carefully out of bed, not wanting to wake Tala, unsure of how long he'd been asleep. He'd had as little sleep as me over the last week, getting up with me every time my body misbehaved.

In the bathroom, I shut the door before turning on the light. I peed and then sat for a bit, trying to decide whether I was going to be sick or if I was hungry. The two feelings weren't dissimilar and needed a little thought.

"Frenchie? Frenchie, where are you?" Tala called out, sounding groggy.

My eyes widened as I glanced down, cupping my belly when the blobs seemed to push against the wall of muscle, reacting to hearing Tala.

The door burst open, and Tala stood gloriously naked. "What is it? Are the babies comin'?" His alarm would have been funny if not for how my blobs were reacting.

"Come here."

I'd barely made the request when he was on his knees in front of me. I reached for his hand and placed it on my belly. "Talk."

His brows shot up his forehead, his gaze on where I'd placed his hand. "About wh—" The hand trembled against my skin. "Are they...movin' in there?"

I was hard-pressed not to laugh at the wonder on his face, despite the alarm in his voice. "Yes. Talk to them. They like the sound of your voice. I think they know you're their daddy."

"They do?"

I nodded, struggling not to shed a tear for the sheer pleasure he wasn't able to contain.

He frowned. "What should I say? Do you think they can understand what I'm sayin'? Shit...oh fuck...damn. No, I didn't mean that. Don't listen to Daddy."

He was too cute for words rambling at my belly. I wasn't sure how long he crouched in front of me talking about...cars, but my ass was numb, and I was back to needing to pee again.

"Why don't you go back to bed? I need to pee again and maybe get something to eat."

I got a swift reaction to the thoughts of food from my stomach, and Tala grinned at me, having not removed his hand. "They're hungry."

"They are, it would seem."

He was up and heading out of the bathroom, calling back, "I'll go make them something."

I bit my lip to stop the laughter.

"Don't you mean for me?" I eventually called after him.

All of you.

Chapter Twenty-One

Tala

Meat frying on low heat, I started on the eggs, then put sliced mushrooms and tomatoes in the pan. I checked the time and added more for me, seeing as I'd need to head to work in a couple of hours.

I blew out a breath, stealing myself at how much I didn't want to go. Never in my life had I ever considered shirking my work responsibilities. Frenchie and the blobs were changing things faster than I could blink. And...I couldn't find a thing wrong with it. The feel of movement under my palm when I'd talked was one that was...fucked if I could put it into words. It was monumental, life-alerting. That's what it was.

Last night I'd been determined to get back to Frenchie as quickly as possible. I'd driven without stopping, not letting Doc argue with me about taking a break. I wanted home. I wanted Frenchie in my arms. I'd managed three hours of sleep before I'd woken to find the bed empty. What had come after left a wild fluttering in my chest, one I was sure I was going to have to get used to.

Pups...fuck, I was having a family.

The excitement was still mixed with terror at how real this all was now that I'd felt the blobs move. The trip to see Jem had given me a lot of time to think. Never one to fret over anyone, not even when Father got sick, I couldn't help but stress myself out when I was apart from Frenchie and our blobs. Something he insisted on calling them.

I chuckled, turning to grab a cloth. I caught my reflection in the glass and stared, not quite believing it was me. I stepped closer to the glass, examining my face. It registered slowly how different I felt. I'd been grumpy for so damn long. It was a shocker to feel something different. My potato was a game-changer.

The sizzling meat brought my attention back to what I was doing. I checked the eggs hadn't burned, stirring them to make sure they didn't stick to the bottom of the pan. Watching the eggs, I considered the trip. It had been an eye-opener, that's for sure. For one, Jem had been a lot more forthcoming when he found out Frenchie was pregnant. The old shifter didn't hide how damn pleased he was that things had worked out. He wasn't so cocky when he heard that Russ wasn't happy and wanted to return, unmated. He couldn't, and we even spoke with one of the elders. Frenchie was right about them. They'd been none too happy with what Jem had done. But they were adamant that no potato could return once past the boundary lands.

It was a fucked up mess, and I'd yet to share that with Russ and Olowin. Olowin had been keeping out of Russ's way, which wasn't helpful when Frenchie insisted that he come with us to the packhouse. The pack was still unaware of the situation with Olowin. However, if he continued to turn into me, a grumpy asshole, then someone was bound to figure it out.

Thankfully that was not my problem. I had more pressing issues. Like how unique my mate was during pregnancy. His kind was able to shift while pregnant and could give birth in their potato form. I'd tried not to think about that, the idea of Frenchie...

No, don't do it.

Don't do what?

Think about food when you're hungry. The lie burned my tongue, and my wolf whined. I cursed, realizing I must have projected my thoughts with the alarm coming from my little potato.

You're fibbing to me. I can tell. "What aren't you telling me?" The latter was said as he came into the kitchen naked and very distracting. The pale and drawn face stopped me from considering doing anything other than finishing breakfast.

When I didn't immediately answer, he tilted his head to the side and widened his eyes. I hunched under the silent accusation. "Sorry. I was telling myself not to think 'bout you givin' birth."

He walked toward me, eyeing me as if he was checking for truth. Seemingly happy I was being truthful, his arms slid around my waist, and he rested his head in the middle of my chest. His soft curls brushed against my skin. "I'm worried too. Did the meeting with Doc Picker and Jem not go well?"

His fear was hard to think past. "It went okay, I think."

I ran a reassuring hand up his naked back, pleased when he tightened his hold and made a cute little sniffle noise. "Doc has some avenues to explore. Potatoes can give birth in both human and shifter form."

There was a big sigh. "I'm not sure the little blobs are going to come out of my skin when I'm a potato. They're already quite big. And that they're pups, not potatoes—"

"You're sure? Doc Picker wasn't sure about what they'd be."

"I feel it. I can't explain it. They might have some of my qualities, but they are pups. How long do wolf pregnancies last? A potato doesn't grow this fast." He pulled back and slid a hand between us to cup his slightly swollen belly.

"Around sixty-three days. Some longer, some shorter. Or that's what Doc said when we were talkin' on the way back. That will make them Christmas babies." I really loved the idea of that. "All I want for Christmas is a Fingerling," I joked.

His giggles were pure joy. "You've already got that."

I tugged him back in and rested my chin on his head. "Yes, I do."

We stood like that until the scent of burning eggs reminded me what I'd been doing. "Fuck."

There were more giggles as he eyed the pan I'd recused from the heat. The yellow and black mix smelled awful. "I'll make some more."

"Nah, my blobs like the smell of those. We'll eat it."

My nose wrinkled in disgust. "Seriously?" I looked at his belly. "They want this shit?"

The nod was immediate, his hand reaching for the pan. "I'll eat it out of the pan."

With that, he took it to the counter, got a fork, and started to eat as if he'd never seen food before, moaning around a full mouth.

All I could see in my head was him bent over the toilet bringing back up that congealed mess. I bit back a sigh and finished plating the rest of the food.

He sat back, having cleared his plate before I'd even made a dent in my food. He rubbed at his belly, a contented smile on his face, which was no longer pale. "Can you tell me what else Jem and Doc Picker had to say?"

I swallowed my mouthful of food. "There isn't much else to say. Doc Picker recommended we fill up the back of the truck with soil. His one bit of advice was that you need to be in the dirt to give birth." The idea was...fuck knows, but Doc had said we'd heed the advice regardless of how we'd do things when Frenchie went into labor. Two different species mixed mating wasn't uncommon.

What was uncommon was Frenchie's kind and animals. There was nothing documented on this happening before, so we were walking around in the damn dark. "He wasn't helpful in regard to your heat."

"This was mentioned before."

"Yeah, the time you're most fertile and can get pregnant. Omegas have a heat every month."

"And you're worried 'cause mine has started early? Not that I actually know what it is or how it's supposed to feel. You know I was a virgin."

"I'm told you get uncontrollable urges to mate that can last for a day or two."

Frenchie's head tipped back, and he roared with laughter. My heart fluttered at the sight of him glowing with radiance in the lights. "I feel that way all the time with you. How do I tell the difference?" he spluttered past the giggles that weren't dying down.

I shrugged, immensely pleased, as was my wolf, who was preening at the compliment. "No clue. Doc is gonna give us a chart thing to keep check once you've had the blobs."

His eyes twinkled with mirth. "Yeah, that might be handy if we want to avoid a house full."

My wolf yipped with excitement, and I gulped in panic. "Two is enough."

"I come from a big family."

His face and thoughts gave nothing away. My stomach dipped alarmingly. "Do you want a big family?" The air somehow got stuck inside me and refused to budge as the seconds ticked past and Frenchie chewed his lower lip between his teeth. His brows furrowed.

After what felt like an eternity, he shook his head. The air hissed through my teeth. *Thank fuck!*

"I want to have the time to be a good daddy to my blobs. There never seemed to be enough time for all of us."

There was sadness coming from him, and I got up, the food forgotten, to scoop him into my arms. The weight of him in my arms was perfect, as was the little noise of contentment he made when he nuzzled into the side of my neck. "We'll make the time to be a...family."

His hand ran over the hair in the center of my chest, love flowing from him. "We will."

Chapter Twenty-Two

Frenchie

"Ooh, that's cold." I shivered as Doc poured gel on my hugely swollen belly that moved in the most peculiar way. The blobs appeared to move away as if sensing what was coming as Doc pressed the probe where he'd put the gel, rubbing it over the taut skin.

Tala squeezed my hand to the point he cut off the circulation, his eyes never moving from the ultrasound machine sitting next to the examination couch. "Wow, they've grown a lot in a week."

"Tell me about it," I complained when one of the blobs pressed down on my bladder. The urge to pee came swiftly. "You're gonna have to stop. One of them is pressing on my bladder. I need to pee."

"You just went when we left the house," Tala pointed out, not so helpfully. His smile was indulgent and set my teeth on edge.

"That might be the case, but you try dealing with something deciding to play a game of squash the bladder. A bladder that now feels like the size of a pea being flattened by a large foot. Try that, and then tell me you don't need to pee every five goddamn minutes," I grumped. Tala said nothing.

The traitor's lips twitched as he motioned for Doc to stop, then helped me roll off the couch.

Back five minutes later, sniffling and feeling out of sorts, Tala helped me to settle on the couch so we could restart the routine of Doc checking the progress of the blobs. The screen showed the two blobs had indeed grown considerably since our last visit. We were a week from Christmas, and I'd a feeling Tala was going to get an early Christmas gift.

It wasn't any one thing, more a sense that my body was preparing itself for something. The last couple of days, I'd needed to spend extra time sitting outside in the dirt. Tala had made a huge wooden box for the back of the house and put half the soil he'd got from home in it. It was the only place I was finding any peace at the moment, which stopped the anxiety creeping up on me when I thought about how the two blobs were going to get out of my body.

Tala leaned in and kissed the top of my head. "It's gonna be fine."

The snarky side of me that had appeared over the last few weeks wanted to slap Tala upside the head for being ridiculous. "For you, yes. You're not the one who is going to push these two rather large blobs out of an orifice that is way smaller than the circumference of their heads." I'd done nothing but calculate the size of their bodies versus the size of my ass!

He visibly paled and hunched in the seat. I wanted to feel sorry for him, but the reality that this was going to happen, and soon, wouldn't let me.

"Your body will adjust."

I narrowed my gaze on Doc. "Are you tellin' me there'll be no pain? That they'll slip right out without an issue?"

None of us were clear on exactly how it was going to work. The research Doc had done was fruitless, though it had given him a list of other vegetables that were shifters. At the time, Tala's anxiety levels had gone through the roof, making me and the blobs very unhappy. We'd spent several hours in the soil, working on calming him and the blobs down. It had worked well for him these last two weeks. But it appeared we'd swapped places as the time drew nearer. I couldn't seem to stop the panic from sneaking up and overwhelming me, like now.

"No, I ain't sayin' that. Birthin' is painful. There is no escaping the contractions that help to push the pups out."

I lifted my free hand. "Stop. I don't want to hear it."

Both wolves' expressions looked amused, and I slumped on the bed, resisting having a hissy fit that I'd hate myself for later. "Let's get this over with, or else I'll need to pee again."

Out on the street half an hour later, I nodded to several folks as we walked down the sidewalk back to where the truck was parked. Tala clutched me to his side, his scowl aimed at anyone who looked in our direction. I swallowed a sigh.

Since the pack had found out that I was pregnant, their acceptance level had improved dramatically. I'd made friends with a couple of the omegas who were sweet and kind. They'd been knitting and bringing me gifts for the blobs. It had been a while, Cain informed me, since there'd been anyone pregnant in town, which brought with it a level of excitement that I hadn't predicted. Neither, it seemed, had my mate when the pack members started to drop by to check in on me. Tala might smile more around me, but he was still grumpy with everyone else.

I'd tried to explain it was good for us to have the pack support, but that fell on deaf ears. Especially when he'd required Nomad and Tundra to come and price out the cost of adding an extension to the house. More pack members had descended on us to help get the house ready, most giving up their free time. With Russ living with us, we had no extra bedroom for the blobs. Not that we needed one right away as they'd be in our room to start with. To that end, we'd bought two cribs and sat one on each side of the bed. Ready for...

"I need...ice cream."

Tala stopped walking, a look of indulgence appearing. "Okay. What flavor do you want me to get?"

"No, I need to see what the blobs want, so I'll come with you into the store," I said firmly, not wanting to argue.

The resigned stare slipped into place as he directed me across the road and into the store.

The place wasn't too busy and Onai, a friendly omega who'd befriended me, waved from the counter. "What you after today, Frenchie?"

At the two pack meetings I'd attended, I'd registered the pecking order in the pack, and with it, I'd learned, for the moment, to hold my tongue on certain things. The last pack meeting the week before was a prime example. Alarick had been rude to Onai, who was just adding his opinion to what was being discussed. At the time, no one had stepped in and told Alarick his behavior wasn't acceptable. Olowin, who seemed a fair alpha, didn't appear to notice that not all pack members were treated as equals. The omegas were definitely at the bottom of the pile for respect. How, I couldn't understand, when they were the ones that created continuity for the pack with their fertility. I'd learned a lot. I wasn't an omega or a beta. Heck, I wasn't sure what I really was, but even the elders at home treated everyone as equal, even if they had archaic ideas.

Due to the hormones, I wasn't always able to filter what came out of my mouth. I'd spent a lot of time recently biting my tongue. My reactions could be a little over the top, and I didn't want to come off as hysterical, not when it mattered. The plan was to wait to talk to Olowin once I'd had the blobs. In the meantime, I'd been trying to encourage the single omegas to stand up for themselves, and Onai was one of them.

"Ice cream, though now I think I need something else to go with it."

Tala stiffened next to me.

Now that the vomiting had stopped, it appeared I could eat absolutely anything without an issue. My food selections, at times, had become a little bizarre. The cravings were something Tala didn't enjoy when it involved mixing food groups, such as last week's craving for raw vegetables covered in chocolate sauce and dipped into mayonnaise. I know he'd spoken to Doc about it. I had as well. Worried that there was something wrong with the blobs, he'd assured me that it was normal and to just eat what I wanted, so I was.

I wandered off down the aisle, leaving a worried-looking Tala. When I walked back, arms full and grinning, he sighed. A huge block of cheese was tucked next to the strawberry ice cream tub. I also had a packet of sprinkles for the ice cream and a jar of peanut butter.

"Together?"

The growling coming from my stomach answered for me. "Maybe we should buy a bowl and spoon so I can eat it in the truck?" I suggested walking to the counter where Amarock, a quiet alpha who tended to say very little during pack meetings, was being served.

He nodded, eyed what I had in my arms, then picked up the grocery sack Onai had just filled. A hint of a smile appeared. "Let's hope you don't get sick in the truck."

"Oh, I'll be fine. The sickness stopped a couple of weeks ago. How are you, Amarock? And how's your leg?" He was a woodcarver, and the chainsaw he'd been using to cut a large chunk of wood had slipped and taken a chunk out of his leg. I'd popped in to get my vitamins when he'd hobbled into the pharmacy looking for something to help finish the healing his shift hadn't been able to. Why he hadn't gone to Doc was beyond me. He'd been adamant his wolf had healed the majority of his injury and that he didn't need Doc. Worried, I'd gotten him to come to the house and gave him some of my soil to see if the healing properties would work on him.

He shook his left leg. "Healed up nice. Thanks for the soil. It did the trick."

"What's this?" Tala asked, appearing with a spoon and bowl in his hands. His tone indicated he was majorly pissed, not that I could figure out why.

Dropping what I held onto the counter, I swung to face Tala, wobbling when my belly left me off-kilter. I grabbed for the countertop and scowled. "I gave Amarock some soil to see if it would help his leg. He cut himself with a chainsaw." I shuddered, recalling the large, jagged scar on his thigh.

There was a fierce growl, and Tala's wolf flashed in his eyes. "What were you doing showing your leg to my mate?"

The quiet alpha didn't so much as flinch at the alpha power radiating off Tala, but Onai was a completely different matter. The poor omega cowered back, his head tilted in submission, his gaze down.

"Stop that. You're upsetting Onai for no reason. I've seen every pack member naked, or have you forgotten that? The whole damn town attends the monthly meeting, and most of them come in their wolf form. This means when they shift, they aren't dressed." I glanced at Amarock, who was watching us with fascination.

"I asked Amarock to let me see his leg to determine how much soil he might need." My hands went to where my waist had once been, and I tapped my foot in frustration. "I was helping one of the pack members. Isn't that what Olowin says is essential?" I'd made every effort to learn about the pack and what it was to be a contributing member.

The grimace remained, but his shoulders relaxed. "Maybe. But I don't want you inviting pack members into our home and getting them to strip off. I don't like it."

The level of petulance was laughable, but I didn't give in. "I'm not promising that. If someone needs my help, then I'm gonna offer it, so get over yourself." I pointed to the counter and gave Onai a wry smile Tala couldn't see. "Can you ring these up, please?"

Chapter Twenty-Three

Tala

Releasing a breath, I reached for the ignition key and twisted it. The throaty roar of the engine had a smile spreading over my face. I had two days to spare before Christmas, and I'd finally completed the car. This one had taken longer than I'd planned with all the interruptions and doctor's appointments for Frenchie. I wasn't complaining, though some of our customers were. I'd told Olowin if they didn't like it, they could go elsewhere.

All the hours I used to work were a distant memory. I'd cut back by half over the last few weeks. The fact was, I hated being away from Frenchie, which in turn upset my wolf, who couldn't understand why I didn't let Frenchie come to work with us if I needed to be in the auto shop. As Frenchie had decided not to take the risk of shifting, and I wasn't prepared for him to be around a busy auto shop when he needed to keep his feet up, he stayed home. His legs had started to swell right along with his belly. He constantly complained about being the size of a house and ungainly, having lost his center of gravity. He was a disaster waiting to happen, one I wanted to wrap in cotton wool to keep safe.

"Fuck, look at him smilin' again. It's freakin' me the fuck out," Redin mumbled to Cain.

I shouted out the car door, hearing every word. "You want me to go back to bein' a miserable, grumpy fucker?"

Redin dropped his gaze. "It's weird, and it doesn't suit you."

Cain gave him a little nudge. "Don't be silly. He looks happy. What's wrong with that? I can't wait to find my mate."

"Yeah, right. Who'd want to mate with you?" Redin bitched nastily.

It was something I was starting to notice more after Frenchie started to point it out and complain to me about how the omegas were treated. "Don't talk to Cain like that. Be more respectful."

The only sound to be heard in the auto shop was the engine running. Slowly, I got out of the car after switching off the engine. Every eye in the place was aimed in my direction. Tension filled the air, and a moment later, Olowin appeared out of his office. His senses were as acute as mine, so I'm sure he'd have heard the conversation.

Redin glanced at Cain, his lip curled up in disgust, a meanness that was common for him appearing. "He's an omega," he spat out.

My attention turned to my brother when I felt his fury. One he didn't hide as he strode toward where Redin and Cain remained standing. "He's a member of this pack. All pack members deserve respect. You seem to have an issue with this,

Redin. I warned you once before. There are no second chances here."

The anger lashed out with each word he spoke, hitting its target as Redin immediately offered his submission.

"Sorry," Redin muttered.

Olowin had him by the throat and easily lifted the beta from the floor. "If you say it, then you need to mean it. Do you think I can't feel the lack of sincerity? You're a disgrace."

"I'm sorry," he choked out past the hand holding his throat in a punishing grip. He swayed in the air, his eyes bulging out of their sockets.

Olowin's fingers flexed, his knuckles whitening further before he dropped Redin back to the floor where the wolf rubbed at his marked throat. "I've been too lenient." The silence was deafening at the harshness of Olowin's voice, a harshness that was a rarity. "You have an hour to pack up your possessions and leave town." There were gasps, but no one said a word. Olowin spun around, and Cain scurried away from Redin, who seemed shocked into stillness.

The phone in my pocket started to vibrate just when a sensation of pain tugged at my stomach and weakened my knees. "Olowin," I called in a panic, pulling out the phone when the pain finally let me breathe easier.

He returned to me, ignoring Redin, who slunk backward toward the door. "What is it?"

"I think it's the blobs."

Olowin lost a little of his color as I answered the call to hear Russ babbling. "Come home...there...oh shit...come...now."

There was a cry in the background as another sweeping pain came through my link with Frenchie.

I panted and bent forward, gripping the phone as I tried to stop myself from crying out.

"What's wrong with you?" Olowin demanded as he put a supporting arm around me to hold me up.

"I'm getting hit with Frenchie's pain. He must be in labor. You'll need to drive me home. I'll never make it alive with what he's bombarding me with. Cain, call Doc and tell him to head to my house."

Frenchie, I'm coming. Hang on.

"Gotcha," Cain called out.

A quick nod, and I staggered outside to my truck with Olowin. Once inside, I started to count the time between the pains.

We'd barely gotten to the edge of town when Olowin suggested, "Why not block him and shift? You'd get home faster."

"No, I need to know he's okay. He's not talkin' to me right now. I think he's gone to get in the soil. He doesn't feel as—" The next words were cut off by another wave of pain. The wall of my stomach muscles clenched so damn tight I thought I was torturing myself by lifting a car by myself. Holy fuck, why did anyone ever want to get pregnant more than once? This was...

Tala...Tala

The panic was real, and my wolf pushed hard at me to shift. Teeth clenched, I tried to reason with him that I couldn't help in my wolf form. He listened, but I was convinced it wouldn't take much for him to break the hold I had when I was suffering right along with Frenchie.

I'm nearly there. The Doc is coming.

Sweat coated my skin by the time Olowin pulled up in front of the house. I was out of the truck before he had a chance to park. Running in through the open door, I ran through the house that looked as if the Christmas fairy had vomited over everything. Frenchie had gone a little wild, and I hadn't had the heart to argue when he got so much fun out of making the place...sparkle.

"Frenchie? Frenchie, I'm here." Out through the back of the house, my legs wobbled at the sight of Frenchie, naked, on all fours, blood-smeared dirt covering his lower body as he rocked back and forth, mewling like a distressed animal caught in a trap. His ass was exposed, and...

I swallowed and looked away, my feet tripping over the step to get in the dirt box. In my haste to get to him, I didn't notice Russ crouched at the side of him until I was kneeling beside Frenchie, and he started to babble. "It happened so fast. One minute he wanted watermelon covered in cream cheese, the next he was howling and stuff was running down the backs of his legs." Russ shuddered.

I ran a hand over Frenchie's back as it rippled, and he panted, mewling and cursing up a storm. "It's okay. I'm here."

The glare he aimed at me after he stopped swearing would have made a lesser wolf cower. It was a good thing I was already kneeling.

"This is all your fault," he rasped.

"I'm sorry," I offered placatingly.

His eyes narrowed. "Next time, it'll be you doing this!"

I gulped and kept the *fuck no, hell would freeze over first* comment to myself. Alphas, as far as I was aware, and prayed, weren't able to conceive.

Back to rocking, Frenchie started to whimper. My stomach muscles started to spasm, alerting me to his next contraction. Going on instinct, I massaged his lower back with one hand while stroking his rippling belly with the other. I uttered useless words, hoping they'd soothe him. When he didn't turn the air blue, I took that as a good sign. I cringed at what was dripping into the soil as one after another contraction hit, each one stronger than the last.

My clothes were glued to my body by the time I heard and smelled Doc. He appeared, carrying a bag, and stopped next to Olowin, who was standing at the side of the box watching, with a rather green tinge to his face.

Out of breath after the last contraction, Frenchie hardly had enough energy to glance at

Doc as he spoke. "As soon as they're born, Tala, you'll need to shift so the pups can do the same."

"What, you didn't mention this before?" Frenchie gasped.

His flushed and feverish face showed signs of distress. A wave of panic came with it, and I worked to soothe him. "The blobs just need to bond with my wolf."

He didn't get a chance to say more when the next contraction made him arch and scream so loud it made my eardrums ring and my wolf recede.

"They're coming," he grunted, his face going purple as he appeared to push his ass down into the dirt, squatting.

I wanted to pull him up, a terror building so strong that he was going to suffocate the blobs that I barely noticed the aching pain in my clenched teeth. As if sensing I was about to do something, Doc put a restraining hand on my shoulder. "Let him be. He's following his instincts."

My wolf snarled and snapped at the hand.

Olowin charged forward, using his alpha power to get me to focus. "Look! Look at Frenchie."

Russ started to cry as he stared down at the soil.

There in the dirt were two perfect, tiny babies. My throat closed up with the strength of emotions that caused tears to blind me. Frenchie looked at me and grinned. "We did it. Look how beautiful they are, Tala."

"Shift, Tala," Doc demanded, interrupting my moment with Frenchie.

My wolf, happy to be taking part, didn't need any more encouragement. There was no time to strip as my clothes tore and my wolf emerged. He yipped excitedly, lowering his nose and sniffing the babies. He licked at them, then nudged them while Frenchie sat back in the soil.

He stroked his trembling hand down the side of my furry flank. "Look at what we did."

My wolf lifted its head and howled, letting everyone know how proud he was. The babies wriggled in the dirt before seeming to figure out what to do. Both shifted with ease. One was dark brown, the other a lighter shade with flecks of gold through his fur.

Cleaning them, my wolf only stopped when he was satisfied, then lay down in the dirt and curled his huge body protectively around the two pups, making a noise that was all contentment.

Our wolves.

Frenchie's hand tightened in my wolf's fur as he came closer. "Ours."

Chapter Twenty-Four

Frenchie

I'd had so much fun decorating the Christmas tree, its lights now twinkling in the evening twilight. The soft, warm air coming through the open windows brought with it the scent of roasted Christmas nuts. I glanced up from my lounging position on the couch where I'd been for the last two hours with Togo and Paco, who were exhausted after all the Christmas excitement.

"Are they asleep?" Tala asked as he came in carrying a small, wrapped box in his hand. He'd been to see off Olowin, who'd come for Christmas dinner, which Russ had cooked. The tension between the two of them seemed to have eased a little, and I hoped they'd found some sort of middle ground, now that Russ was staying with us permanently. Tala wasn't totally on board with having Russ living with us, although for once, he'd kept his thoughts to himself. He wasn't always able to fully shield his displeasure at having to share our home.

Whatever I'd expected about how Tala would be when the pups arrived, it wasn't this super laid-back person who cooed and spoke in a baby voice. No, that was the last thing I'd considered. It was too cute for words.

"They are, but for how long, who knows?" Togo, who looked more like me, appeared more energetic than his sibling. Paco was all Tala and seemed content to eat and sleep the day away. They were both currently lying on my chest, one cradled in each arm, having fallen asleep when Tala had been talking to Olowin outside.

Tala placed the box on the table next to the formula bottles and lifted my legs carefully so as not to disturb the babies, placing them over his thighs. It had only been two days since the birth, and I was exhausted. My body still wasn't sure what to make of what it had been through. The muscles in my ass seemed to have returned to normal after some time in the dirt, but my time out in my dirt box had been limited by the sheer number of visitors. I was hoping, now that Christmas was over, we'd get some alone time, or nearly alone time with Russ in the house.

I eyed the gaily wrapped box, then Tala. "Is that another gift for the babies?"

There was a huge mountain of presents that would require a room all of their own to house. Nomad had assured me that once New Year was out of the way, work would resume on the extension, which they had been making quick progress on. Just not quick enough for the pups.

"Nope." Tala's tangled mess of hair shook about his head. A pink hue spread over the bridge of his nose. A hand ran up and down one of my legs as he stared at the pups.

"What is it?" My brows rose when he licked his lips in a nervous gesture. One I wasn't used to seeing from him.

He reached over my legs to pick up the box and offer it to me.

I giggled and eyed the top of the two babies' heads. "My hands are a little full right now. Who gave it to us? You can open it, can't you?"

His Adam's apple bobbed repeatedly, and a sense of...unease bled from him. "It's for you. I bought you a Christmas present."

"You did," I said in a choked whisper. "I never got you anything. I don't have any money."

He scowled, and everything in my world was right again. "I told you what's mine is yours," he huffed out loudly. "I'll get a bank card for you."

My lips quivered. "Thank you."

He waved the box at me. "Do you want me to open this, or do you want to wait until after you put the pups down?"

The sense I got from him was that he wanted me to see what was inside, so I answered, "You open it."

Peeling back the paper with care, he revealed a black box with a gold wolf's head on it. "Wolves are all about family, pack, friendships, loyalty, protection, and deep connections." He opened the lid, and lights from the tree made the four wolves' heads in different stones on a leather band gleam.

"Each wolf's head represents a wolf totem." He rubbed his thumb over each of the stones as he spoke quietly. "Emerald is the stone for family. The one you've made for me. Celestite is a spirit guide to protect its wearer. This is for when we're apart. Kambaba Jasper is linked with earth energy, bringing you closer to nature. Perfect for my little potato." The pink across his nose darkened, but he didn't look away as he lifted out the leather band. The stones rocked together gently. "And Pink Kunzite is the stone of love. I'm not good with flowery words like Olowin, and I'll no doubt piss you off more than not." He came forward. "Lift up."

A fluttering started under my breastbone as I sniffed and blinked back my tears at the depth of his feelings, none of which he held back. They were a blessing that filled me. I sat up as much as the babies would allow, tilting my head to allow him to tie the leather thong around my neck.

His breath touched my lips as he pressed the briefest of kisses to them. "Know this. I love you with everything I am. I will die to protect you and our family." The flash of wolf in his eyes reiterated the truth of his words.

I giggled and pressed my nose against his, keeping my tone light. "You were doing so well with the romantic gesture. Then you go and spoil it with talk of dying."

The scowl was back, and I kissed him hard and fast. "Gosh, I love when you scowl at me like that." I sighed and met his gaze, saying in all seriousness, "The same goes. You're mine and the pups. There is nothing I wouldn't do to protect all of you. I might not be a ferocious wolf, but that doesn't mean I won't fight to the death to protect what is mine."

I'd had time to think about the missed opportunity to discuss Leno, and though this wasn't the most ideal time to talk about my suspicions, I didn't think I'd get a better one. "Do you think you could take Paco, and we'll put them down in the cribs? I have something I want to talk about."

The frown came even while he reached to take Paco, who stirred for a second then snuggled into Tala, who got a soppy look on his face. Thankfully, he was distracted from asking anything or probing my thoughts while I considered what to say.

Ten minutes later, with the pups asleep in their cribs, I ran a hand over the wolves' heads, centering myself. Tala walked to the kitchen and grabbed two beers, bringing them to me when I sat down on the sofa. He offered me a bottle, and I took it for something to do with my hands.

He remained silent and watchful.

"You asked me about why I'd mentioned wet dog the night of my first pack meeting, then we got side-tracked." He nodded, his thoughts and face revealing nothing, showing how worried he was. I'd learned to read my mate.

I swallowed to wet my throat without considering taking a drink from the beer I held. "The day I got hurt, I smelled wet dog beforehand."

Tala was off the sofa, his whole body quivering and his wolf right there.

Remember, the pups are sleeping. Don't shout. Shout! Shout!

He shouted the words, and they rattled around my head. I shook my head and got up, placing my bottle down, being led by the panic and erratic thoughts he wasn't able to control.

I'm fine. Look at me. There is nothing for you or your wolf to be concerned about. I'm sorry I've not mentioned this earlier, but we've been a little preoccupied with other things. First the challenge, then the pregnancy. I can feel your need to go, and...well, let's not think about what you want to do.

Do you think Leno hurt you?

Leno is dead, and I can't remember exactly what happened that day. I don't want to accuse a dead wolf of...see, that's the problem. I don't know what I'd be accusing him of. All I know for sure was I scented him outside, then I remember nothing.

The massive chest I was eye level with puffed in and out as if Tala had been running for hours. The bottle in his hand shook. *My wolf scented Leno in the back of the property, but I was too preoccupied with chopping bits of you and eating them to question why. Fuck-it-to-all-hell!*

I pried it from his fingers and placed it next to mine on the cluttered table, not sure he wouldn't send it flying if he continued to hold it. Stepping closer to him, I reached for his hands and opened his arms, allowing me to lay my head on his chest. His body relaxed against me, my energy working to remove his tension. "Tala, I love you."

He growled. "That's a low blow. And don't think I don't feel you letting out all those peaceful vibes on me." The gruffness held a wealth of love that got me smiling. His arms wrapped around me and held tight. "Answer me this one thing, then I'll drop the subject."

I tilted my head back. "What is it?"

"Do you think Leno hurt you on purpose?"

I didn't sigh, though I wanted to. "Yes, yes I do." I laid my head back onto his chest. "I'm not sure why I feel that, but I do."

"It's a damn good thing that he's already dead."

"Yes, well, he is, and he got his just desserts." My belly rumbled. "Talking of desserts, do we have any ice cream left over?"

Tala's body shook before laughter rumbled up his chest, the sound as precious as him. "There is, but please, whatever you do, don't mix it with any crazy shit."

I blushed, recalling every craving he'd helped me indulge. "You're safe. No more crazy, I swear."

His arms tightened, a wide smile on his face. "I don't mind a little crazy when it involves my little Fingerling."

"You know that sounds…"

"Perfect."

Epilogue

Tala

Ever since Olowin had called by the house the week before to talk about tonight's pack meeting, I'd been on edge. I'd known it was only a matter of time before he'd bring up the mating ritual in the wolf circle at the packhouse. I'd managed to put it off, first because of Leno, then Frenchie being pregnant.

They were now three months old and spent so much time as pups, there was no longer an excuse to not come to the pack meeting and officially introduce them to the pack. That meant there was also no need to delay any longer on the mating ritual. I'd argued with Olowin that we'd been mated for over six months and had two pups. What was a ritual gonna prove?

"Stop grumping. You're giving me a headache," Frenchie said as he appeared from the new extension carrying Togo. He had his fingers wrapped in Frenchie's curls, which he loved to play with.

I opened my arms, and Togo wriggled. Frenchie untangled the hand in his hair, handing an excited Togo over. "Dad wins hands-down, doesn't he?" Babbling followed as Togo reached out and stroked my bristly jaw.

"What are you sayin', puddin'?"

Frenchie arched just one brow at me. "Stop callin' him that. You'll give him a complex."

I gently pinched one of Togo's cheeks, which were round and chubby. "He's my puddin', aren't you?" I glanced up from the drooling baby to Frenchie grinning. "Where's Paco?"

"He decided to dirty his diaper because he hates wearing the damn thing, so Russ is changing him."

Paco was showing his alpha traits more every day, and it was like trying to argue with a silent Olowin. "Leave it off. He'll shift the minute we get to the packhouse, so he may as well go naked."

Frenchie rolled his eyes. "Okay, buster, then I'll drive, and he can sit on your knee while you play Russian roulette with him."

I eyed Togo, who sounded as if he was giggling. "You think that's funny, puddin'?" There was more babbling and drool dripped onto the back of my hand.

Russ appeared a second later, looking flustered and disheveled, muttering, "Why do I seem to always be left with Mister Wriggle Bottom."

"Hey, that's my pup you're bein' critical of."

The laughter came from both Frenchie and Russ. Frenchie came over and pinched my nose. "Pot and kettle."

"What does that even mean?" I grumped, not in the least bit annoyed, when Frenchie's eyes sparkled with contagious happiness.

"No clue, I heard Doc say it. Anyway, you've delayed enough. We need to go."

It was then I noticed Frenchie was wearing his original outfit that allowed him to shift fully clothed. "I love you."

He glowed with happiness. "What's not to love?"

I caught the look of sadness on Russ's face before he buried it in Paco's dark curls. There'd been no resolution between him and Olowin. In fact, the pair were actively avoiding each other.

Do you think we should leave Russ and Olowin alone with the boys? See if they can get their shit together?

You think that's a good idea?

Frenchie kept the smile, but there was a heap of worry coming through our link when he responded.

Who knows, but they're both miserable. We could leave them with the pups after the mating ritual.

Frenchie turned away so Russ couldn't see his expression as his shoulders started to shake. *No ulterior motive there.*

There was little downtime, day or night, for us, and that meant getting some alone time where we didn't both collapse in exhaustion was difficult, if not impossible. Not that I was complaining...all right, maybe a little. Tonight was going to be one big lesson in restraint if I didn't want to do all the things I'd been thinking about once my cock was in my mate's mouth.

"Jeez, come on. I've been trying not to think about what's gonna happen. The pups are gonna be present. I don't want to traumatize them with..." He groaned and sent an image that got my body reacting with vigor.

I pointed at him. "I'm on to you."

Russ walked to the door. "Let's go. I'm not sure I'm ready for this either."

At the packhouse, there was a buzz of excitement as the pups, as predicted, had shifted and were chasing after Shrio and Zylo, a beta and an omega, who'd happily shifted to play with them.

The celebration was something Frenchie deserved, and no matter what nerves I felt coming from him, he wanted this, wanted to be fully accepted by the pack.

Frenchie wandered over to talk to Onai and Cain with Russ in tow.

Olowin came and stood silently at my side, his gaze on Russ.

"After the ritual, will you take care of the pups so I can have some alone time with Frenchie."

His head twisted in my direction. "Alone?"

I bit my lip to stop the laughter at how alarmed he sounded, understanding he meant being alone with two pups. "You too scared, brother?"

The scowl was immediate. "No."

"Liar," I said through laughter that I didn't hold back. "It's all right. Russ will help. He's real good with them."

A mask slipped into place, hiding his thoughts. "Can't you get Dad or one of the omegas to help out?"

"Dad has been helping out. You're their uncle. Don't you want to spend time with them?" I added just enough hurt to my voice to guilt him.

His shoulders hunched. "Of course I do."

I grinned at him, cutting him off before he could say more or find an excuse. "Great, then that's figured out. What time are we startin'?"

He glanced about the large, packed room, his eyes narrowing. "There are a couple missing. Let's give it another ten minutes."

There'd been some changes with Frenchie's influence. He had an ability to create harmony, and it was more than his infectious laugh and sunny disposition. The peace that came from his presence in a room had come in handy a time or two when there were a few wolves that remained hostile at the mixed mating. Tonight the hostility levels were low, yet they remained present.

Bertulf and Duko, two betas that had vied for my attention in the past, wandered over. Both were of similar stature, not overly tall but solidly built with powerful upper bodies. Their scent reeked of...*envy*.

Both wolves stopped within a foot of us. As pack protectors, they were part of Olowin's inner circle and had more privileges than others. Bertulf, the mouthier of the two, grinned.

"Never thought I'd see the day you'd let yourself become mated, and to...*a potato*." The latter was choked out past laughter. "That's gonna make the mating ritual...interesting."

The look he swept over Frenchie wasn't in any way appreciative and held a wealth of disdain he wasn't clever enough to conceal.

Duko joined in the laughter, appearing to think that his position in the pack protected him and Bertulf from my wrath.

Fury ran hot and wild from both Olowin and my wolf, who was snarling to be let free to teach these wolves a lesson. Before either of us could react, Frenchie was across the room, leading with his chin. There was a light in his eyes that got my wolf all excited.

Olowin's evil chuckles filled my head. *I'll deal with these two fuckwits after the ceremony. We are not letting anything halt it this time, and that includes this pair. Though I think your mate might have a few words to say first!*

"You think a potato shifter is funny? I suppose it is when you're ignorant of other shifters. I mean, really, wait till you find yourselves mated to say...a green bean..." His smile was so damn bright it eclipsed the sun and moon at once. "Then you'll really have something to laugh about. They are pretty useless, from what I hear."

Frenchie ran a possessive hand up my arm, and my body instantly took notice. "And it must be hard, seeing as you've lost out on any chance to mate to all this deliciousness. I mean, I totally get why you're feelin' bitchy 'bout it. I'd feel a little peeved in your positions too." A pitying gaze swept over them. "Now, if you don't mind, we've got a ritual to get on with."

He gave them both a sassy wink as he took hold of my arm and tugged harder than I was expecting. I went with him to avoid tripping over him and my feet.

The growl that came from Olowin made a smile spread over my face. It appeased my wolf a little as I assured him Olowin would deal with the betas once the ceremony was over. Redin's departure from town had been the talk of the pack, and if anyone had any thought Olowin was a pushover, they now knew differently.

Those standing in front of us parted to let us through and followed as Frenchie led us out of the house.

At the pack circle, he stepped over the stones to face me, a beautiful smile lighting his face. The stones sang when I stepped into the circle. The earth beneath my booted feet felt like the first time I'd got out of the truck on my way to Potatoville. There was no time to reflect on that because Frenchie's hands came up and cupped my cheeks, bringing my head down close enough for him to kiss me. His lips were gentle and coaxing. I groaned and deepened the kiss, encouraging him to part his lips. I swept my tongue into his mouth, the sweet taste of him polar opposite to the dirty images he was sending to me.

Damn, you gotta stop, or I'm gonna have you on the ground with my cock buried in your ass before we start.

I'm not opposed to that idea.

You'd tempt the devil!

He giggled. *Only you.*

"It seems these two are in a rush." Olowin's voice was full of amusement. *Can you at least wait for me to make this official?*

Frenchie jerked back, his mouth hanging open. *I can hear you! Holy cow.* He glanced down at the ground. *It's the circle. It's magic.*

Olowin nodded. *This place is sacred to wolves and holds the power of those generations that came before us. You hearing me shows our ancestral spirits' acceptance of this mating.*

Frenchie sniffed loudly, his eyes sheened with tears.

No, don't you dare start crying. My wolf hates it.

The wet chuckle came with an eye roll.

"Shall we start?" Olowin asked, quietening those around us.

"Yes."

"Let's."

The rush of the air over my fur was glorious. Running in my wolf form was never more freeing than with Frenchie nestled on my tongue. The second he'd bitten me, my wolf had surfaced to claim our mate. Dual bites witnessed by the pack, Frenchie had shifted, and my wolf had picked him up and was off running into the forest. The brightness of the full moon guided the way.

Olowin's shouts were ignored, with my little potato wiggling with the thrill of what had just happened. There were so many thoughts, all of them involving what he wanted to happen next. All of which my wolf was happy to let me oblige, as long as it was away from the pack. I was in full agreement with where he was heading.

Water hitting rock overrode the sounds of the night forest as we came to a halt at the waterfall. My wolf lay Frenchie on a rock, the same one I'd sat on months earlier complaining about my little potato. He licked Frenchie, nosing him until the potato became a man. He reached out and stroked a hand over my wolf's snout. "So beautiful, and all mine."

My wolf lowered its head, pushing into the gentle touch, relishing the connection. The love was strong and powerful, matching both sides of me perfectly. My wolf receded with that acknowledgment. Before I'd taken a step forward,

Frenchie held up his hand. "Let me at least get my clothes off first."

Throwing my head back, laughter boomed out, making trees rustle and critters scuttle away.

"I'm not taking any chances," he grumbled, sounding a little like me.

Naked and fully aroused, my laughter turned to a moan of delight as the moonlight bathed his lean body. The wolf heads hanging around his neck clinked together as I picked him up and cupped his ass. His arousal scented the air.

Our lips met in a hungry kiss, and his cock pressed eagerly against mine as he rocked his hips, the potent fragrance of his slick becoming intoxicating. Turning, I staggered back until I felt the rock behind my legs. I sat down and groaned as Frenchie shifted position, attempting to impale himself on my cock.

His mouth hungrily nipped at my lip. The taste of my cum lingered from the mating ritual. "Fuck me. God, I need you inside me." He wriggled, his thighs gripping my legs, and before I could register what his intention was, he lifted himself up and then surged down.

My cock met no resistance as it sank into his willing body. The tight, wet heat caused shudders of desire to ripple through me, nearly tipping us off the rock. Hands threaded into my hair, his mouth never leaving mine as he started to fuck me.

The aggressiveness, not something I'd thought my wolf would tolerate, was met with giddy delight. He was lying on his back, fucking panting. A little disconcerted, I didn't move.

Frenchie nipped at my lower lip, making it sting and sending jolts of desire to my throbbing cock. "Want you so bad. Fuck me! Fuck me hard, make me feel you...*everywhere*."

His words pulled me from my immobility. Like this, there was no way I could resist him. His hair tumbled about his head, his eyes aglow with need. Thrusting up, my hold on his hips became punishing as I gave Frenchie everything he demanded.

"Yes," he hollered.

His hands tugged hard enough on my hair that pain shot into my scalp. "Ride me. Show me how much you want me," I growled, my wolf wanting this as much as me.

On the next thrust, the man on my lap squeezed so hard my eyes felt like they were crossing. The pain and pleasure created sensory overload, and my cock ached in the best way possible.

Frenchie slid his cock over my abdomen and whined. "More, dammit. More."

The frantic slap of skin on skin drove my ass down hard on the rock beneath me. It registered, in some part of my brain, that I'd have a bruise on my ass the next day. I continued to give my mate everything he wanted. Delicious sparks of pleasure spread like hot caresses from my ass, through my balls, and into my cock.

I brought Frenchie to me, kissing him deeply. He sucked on my tongue and stars exploded everywhere as my body was held captive in the depth of a tsunami. Cum exploded from my body in long, hot spurts that got my wolf howling in my head while Frenchie cried out into my mouth. I captured the sound as cum scented the air, warm, wet heat spreading between our sweat-slicked skin.

We clung to each other, neither willing to let go or stop kissing as the life I'd once thought I'd wanted was replaced with something amazing...*Frenchie, my very own little Fingerling.*

To claim a free book My Forever Love, sign up to my newsletter and to gain access to all the bonus chapters.

Other books by the author

Standalone
When Fake Changed Everything
Christmas beyond Christmas
The Elves and the Bondage Daddy (Grim and Sinister
Delights Book 5)

Series
The Potters Creek Series
A Christmas Wish (book one)

The App Series
The App: Daddy kink (book one)
The App: Littles (book two)
The App: Puppy play (book three)

The Flamingo Bar Series
Always More (book one)
The Little Side of Me (book two)
3 Is the Magic Number (book three)

La Trattoria Di Amore Series
Puzzle Pieces (book one)
Dominated but not Subdued (book two)
Made to Submit

The Playroom Series
Mine, Body and Soul: Part One
Mine, Body and Soul: Part Two

Mine, Body and Soul: Part Three
Ferron's Journey: Damaged Part One (book four)
Ferron's Journey: Hidden Part Two (book five)
Ferron's Journey: Revelation Part Three (book six)
Mine, Body and Soul Trilogy
Ferron's Journey Trilogy
Spinoff Love's Heart Print

Dark River Stone Collective Series
The Light Beneath the Dark (Book One)
When Darkness Turns to Light (Book Two)

The Billionaire Playground Series
Property of a Billionaire (Book one)
Reluctant Billionaire (Book two)
Billionaire's Muse (Book three)

The Manx Cat Guardians Series
Where it all Began: Origins (Book 1)
Seeing Beyond the Scars (Book 2)
Destiny Collides Past and Present (Book 3)
Searching for a Soul to Love (Book 4)
The 12 Disasters of Christmas (Book 5)
Laws of Attraction (Book 6)
The Teacher's Boy (Book 7)
Boxset

Audio Books
Mine, Body and Soul, Part One: The Playroom Series
Mine, Body and Soul, Part Two: The Playroom Series

Mine, Body and Soul, Part Three: The Playroom Series
Daddy Kink: The App (book one)
Always More: The Flamingo Bar (book one)
When Fake Changed Everything
Ferron's Journey: Damaged Part One
Ferron's Journey: Hidden Part Two
Ferron's Journey: Revelation Part Three

Romance books in a mixed series of M/F and M/M by
the Author under a different pen name Jayne Paton

Smith's Corner

Delilah & Dallas (book one)
Layla & Levi (Book two) August 2021
Ash & Alora (Book three) out October 2021
Fox & Faith (book four) Release date December 2021
Storm & Stone (book five) Release date February 2022
Hunter & Holden (book six) Release date March/April
2022

Crime and Thrillers by the Author under a different
pen name J Paton

Headspace
Chozen: Dark MM Crime Drama (Headspace Book 1)

About the author

Eccentric cake lover who has a passion for words of all kinds. I'm Jayne or JP, I live in the Isle of Man. A tiny place in the Irish sea where all the magic happens. I'm a confessed bookaholic and if I'm not writing I love to snuggle with a book or two...if you catch my drift.

If you're interested in keeping up to date, then I've a few places you can do that, and they're listed below. My website is where you'll find all the different Me's there are, LOL. As I travel this path into the future, I'm going to be writing in different genres so to stop there being any confusion I'll be writing under different pen names.

If you would like to give me any feedback or just have any questions, go ahead and friend me on Facebook, and I would be happy to answer anything. I hope you enjoyed this book and if you would also like to leave a review, then I would love to read your thoughts. Even if you just want to rate it, I'll be grateful 😊

Thank you for being a part of my dream.

Made in the USA
Las Vegas, NV
13 March 2022